SEVEN LITTLE PEOPLE AND THEIR FRIENDS

HORACE E. SCUDDER

THE THREE WISHES

LITTLE Effie Gilder's porridge did taste good! and so it ought; for beside that Mother Gilder made it, and Mother Gilder's porridge was always just right, Effie was eating it on her seat upon the sea-shore in front of her father's house. The sun was just going down and the tide was rising, so that the little waves came tumbling up on the beach, as if they were racing, each one falling headlong on the sand in the scramble to get there first; and then slipping back again, there would be left a long streak of white foam just out of reach of Effie. She was sitting on what she called her chair, but it was a chair without legs or back or arms—only a great flat stone, where she used to come every sunshiny afternoon and eat her bowl of porridge.

It was smoking-hot—that porridge! and she was eating away with a great relish, holding the bowl in her lap and drumming upon it with her drumstick of a spoon. I wish you could have seen her as she sat there, with her hat falling off and the sun touching her hair and turning the rich auburn into a golden colour. But somebody did see her; for just before the sun went down, Effie spied an old man coming along the beach to the place where she sat. "That must be Uncle Ralph," thought she, "coming home from fishing." "No," she said; as he came nearer, "it isn't, it's Granther Allen." "Why no! it isn't Granther; who can it be? what a queer old man!"

By this time the old man had come quite near. He was a very old man. His hair was long and as white as snow; he was so bent over that as he leaned upon his smooth stout cane, his head almost touched the knob on the top of it; and it kept wagging sidewise, as if he were saying "No" all the time. He had on a long grey coat almost the colour of his hair, and it reached down to his feet on which was a pair of shoes so covered with dust that they were of the same colour as his coat; and his hat was the oddest of all! it was very high and peaked, and looked as if it had been rubbed in the flour barrel before he put it on.

This old man came up toward Effie very slowly, his head shaking all the time and his feet dragging one after the other as if he could hardly reach her. Effie began to be frightened, but when he spoke to her it was with such a sweet musical voice that she thought she had never heard anything half so beautiful.

"My little child," said he, "I am very tired; I have come a long way to-day and have had nothing to eat since morning. Will you give me some of your porridge that looks so nice?"

"Oh yes! sir," said Effie, jumping up and giving him the bowl. "But there isn't much left. Won t you come into the house and mother will give you some bread."

"Oh, no! my little girl," said the old man. "I do not need anything more than this porridge to make me strong again;" and as he spoke, he raised himself up and stood as straight as his own smooth stick that his hand hardly rested on; and his head stopped wagging, and he stood there a tall old man with a beautiful face and such a beautiful voice as he asked again:

"What is your name, my little girl?"

"Effie Gilder, sir. And this is my birth-day; I'm six years old to-day."

"Six years old to-day! and what shall I give you, little Effie, on this your birth-day? I love all good little children, and you were good to me to give me your porridge. Little Effie, I am going to let you wish three things, but you may only wish one thing at a time. One thing to-day, and another when your next birth-day comes, and the last when the birth-day after that comes. Now tell me what you wish most of all."

Effie looked at him in wonder. "What! really? have any thing she wanted for the asking?"

"Yes," said the old man; "but you must ask it before the sun goes down."

Effie looked at the sun; it had nearly touched the water and looked like a great red ball, and she thought it would go down, clear, into the water, as she had so often seen it, without any clouds around it.

"I wish,—" said she, "let me see what I wish! oh, I wish that I might go down to the bottom of the ocean and see all the beautiful shells and the fishes, and every thing that's going on down there!" When she said it, the little waves laughed as they came scampering up to her, as if they said—"What a droll idea!"

"You shall go," said the old man, "before many more suns have set. And next year when your birth-day comes round, I will come again for your second wish. Farewell, my little child."

Effie looked at him, and lo! he was quite bent over again, and his head was shaking harder than ever, as if he said "No, no, no," all the while; then she looked at the sun to see it go down, clear, into the water, but about it were clouds of gold and crimson, and the sun just peeped out behind them, as behind bars, for a moment, and then went down covered by the clouds into the black waters; and in a moment or two, as she stood watching, the beautiful clouds were grey and sombre and spread in a long, low line along the horizon.

"Effie! Effie! come into the house!" she heard her mother calling; and there was Mrs. Gilder, standing in the door-way with her gown tucked up around her, and an apron on, which was the most wonderful apron for pockets you ever saw! I should not dare to say how many pockets it had, for fear you would not believe me, but if you had seen how many things she kept in them, you would think with me, that there never was such a wonderful apron.

"Come here, Effie," said she, and diving into one of her apron pockets she pulled out a little parcel. "See what I've brought you from the village for a birth-day present;" and she unrolled the paper and showed her a little candy dog; his body was white, striped blue and red, and his short tail stood straight up, which was more than the little dog could do, for when he was put on the table, instead of standing on his four legs like respectable dogs, he fell over on his side. Effie took the dog, but did not seem half so glad to get it as her mother thought she would, and even forgot to thank her for it.

"Oh, mother!" said she, "did you see that real old man just now, with such long white hair, and a white coat that came way down to his heels, and his head went just so"—shaking her own, "and oh! he told me I might have any thing I wanted, and I said I wanted to go down to the bottom of the ocean, and he said I should, and he's coming again on my next birth-day, and I am to wish for something again. Do you think he really can take me to the bottom of the sea?"

"Nonsense! child. It's some old crazy man. I wonder you didn't run away from him. Come into the house, it's time for you to go to bed. And bring your dog along with you. You mustn't eat it. It's only to play with."

"I hate that nasty little dog!" said Effie, and her pretty face became twisted into a pucker, "and I don't want to go to bed."

"Tut, tut! Puss," said Father Gilder, who was smoking his pipe by the fire. "What! naughty on your birth-day? I thought you were going to be good always after this. I guess she's tired, mother."

Effie's pouting was crying by this time, and Mother Gilder brought a handkerchief out of another of her pockets, and wiping the child's face, led her to her little cot and put her to bed with the little dog where she could see it when she woke up, lying stiff on his side with his tail straight up in the air.

Father Gilder shook his head. "'T won't do, mother," said he, "we can't have little Effie a cross child. Bless me! why, my pipe's out! where's some tobacco?"

"Here," said Mrs. Gilder, plunging her hand into another of her wonderful apron's pockets and fishing out some tobacco, and then diving into another for matches, filling and lighting her old man's pipe. They looked at the little child lying in her crib, and thought now they would do any thing in the world to make her happy and good. She was fast asleep now, and her little face had become untied—for you know it was in a knot when she lay down—and now she was smiling in her sleep. Perhaps she was dreaming about the old man with the beautiful voice, and thinking she saw him again.

The next day, Effie was playing on the beach, picking up the shells and making little holes in the sand, watching to see the water come up and fill them, when she remembered the old man she had seen the day before, and she said to herself, "I wish he would come and take me down to the bottom of the ocean!" when, lo! just as she had wished it, the queerest little man came walking out of the water to where she stood. He was the funniest looking little man, I'll be bound, you ever saw. He was not more than three feet high, and he had a hump-back—so humped that it looked almost like a wide horn coming out of his back. And he was dressed entirely in green; just as green as sea-weed, and to tell the truth, his clothes were made of sea-weed when you came to look at them closely; all woven of green sea-weed, and on the hump, his coat, which was made to fit it, was stuffed with soft sea grass so that it looked like a cushion. His feet were great flat feet, and his hands were almost as large as his feet; and as for his legs, they were so crooked and so covered with barnacles, that you never would have known them for legs anywhere else. He had on a cap made of seal-skin with two ends bobbing behind.

He came right out of the water and stood before Effie, dripping with wet, and bowing, and smiling, and scraping and twitching his cap, as much as to say, "Your most obedient servant, Miss, and what can I do for you this morning?" and he did say out aloud, "It's all right! Get up there"—pointing to his hump —"and I will carry you down safely, little maiden!"

"But I shall get wet!" laughed Effie.

"Oh, no!" said he, "I'll cover you up." So he stooped down, but he didn't have very far to stoop, he was so short; and she got on top of the hump and held on by the ends of the seal-skin cap that were dangling behind. The little man put his hands in his pockets and pulled out bunches of sea-weed and covered her up with it, and tied her on with long string of sea-grass, until she was quite safe, and then waded straight into the water.

The beach sloped quickly and the little man was short, so that in a few strides the water was up to the hump on which Effie was sitting. Then the little girl began to be frightened and shut her eyes tight, and when she heard the water splashing about them, she wanted to cry out, but she couldn't and held on tight to the bobs of the seal-skin cap. Then she felt the water rushing over their heads, but still the little sea-green man went striding over the ground, putting out his flat hands at his side, as if they were oars, and seeming to push the water away as he went swiftly forward. At first Effie could hear the water overhead, tumbling and rolling about and rising up and down; then it became quieter, and finally it was perfectly still, except when some fish would dart by them, just grazing the hump and disturbing the water a little.

Now, when every thing was so quiet, she began slowly to raise her eyelids a little, until she had her eyes wide open and was staring about her. She seemed to be looking through green glass, and could not see very distinctly, but every once in a while some dim fish would move beside her; and as her eyes got more used to the place, all things became clearer, and soon she saw that on both sides of her and behind, there was a multitude of fishes of all sizes. They swam beside her, the older and bigger ones moving very sedately, and keeping the same order; but the little frisky fishes would tumble around in great glee, and come darting up to Effie, putting their cold noses up to her face and then go racing back, giggling and whipping their tails about in a fine frolic; and the awkward, bungling, good-natured dolphins, would come tumbling in among the steady fishes and make the greatest commotion, almost upsetting little Effie two or three times, and then go bouncing off, shaking their fat sides with laughter. There was an old sword-fish, that seemed to be a kind of special constable, who kept going round and round, pricking the dolphins whenever he got a chance and frightening the little fishes almost out of their senses; as often as he made his appearance, with that long sword of his sticking out, such a scampering as there would be! and how the wee fishes would try to hide behind the dolphins, and how the dolphins would slap them with their fins, and go rolling in among the steady fishes, as if they were the most quiet, well-disposed, respectable fishes that ever were. Oh! how they frolicked and tumbled about the little sea-green man with Effie on his back! Effie shouted and clapped her hands in great glee, and tried to hop up and down on the little man's hump, but she was so tied down that she couldn't, so she kept digging her toes into his back, and twitching the bobs of the seal-skin cap, till he got going at a terrible pace, so fast that it was as much as the fishes and dolphins could do to keep up with him, without playing by the way!

Now, after they had gone what seemed to Effie a great way, every thing became clearer, and the little man shortened his pace and began arranging his cap, which Effie had pulled out of shape, and smoothing down his sea-weed clothes; the fishes all went slowly along in their regular places, only the little fishes behind would teaze the dolphins, and the sword-fish looked as stately as the old fellow could, and gave some serious digs at the dolphins whenever they showed signs of being unruly; and lastly, two or three flying-fish shot off in advance of the rest, and the procession moved slowly on.

"What is coming, I wonder!" thought Effie. Then she looked all about her and over the little man's shoulder to see what was in front; and away off in the distance she saw the dim outline of something that looked like a gate-way. And as they came nearer, sure enough it was a gate-way, and when they came up to it she saw the pillars, made of beautiful white coral, and the gate itself made of a whale's skin, polished and studded with shark's teeth as white as ivory. The little man stopped before the gate, which was shut, and the sword-fish came forward in the most pompous manner, and knocked with his sword upon the coral posts.

"Who comes here?" asked a voice within. "I demand it in the name of the Queen of the Ocean Deeps."

"I come," said the little sea-green man, "I, the servant of the Queen of the Ocean Deeps bearing with me the earth-born child. I crave admittance in the name of the Queen."

At that the gates swung open and the procession moved in. Once through the gate-way, where sat the porter—a hermit crab—the road, paved with lovely shells, wound about, and Effie held her breath to see how beautiful it was. They moved along the shining floor, and by-and-by they came to another gate, more beautiful than the first, where they went through the same form, only the porter within, just before he swung open the doors, said:

"Enter, servant of the Queen of the Ocean Deeps, bearing the earth-born child, and ye his attendants, but let no one enter who does not the bidding of our good-loving Queen." As each one passed in, the porter said:

"When thou comest through this gate,
Leave behind thee sinful hate.
He that can not—let him wait."

And each one answered, else the porter would not have let him in,

"There is no thing in all the sea,
That I or hate or hateth me.
I only hate the sin I flee."

When it came to the little fishes' turn, the old constable sword-fish looked sharply at them, but they answered like the rest in a demure way, with a side wink at the dolphins; those lubberly fellows blundered through somehow, and looked sheepish enough at saying it so poorly. Last of all came the sword-fish, who seemed to feel hurt that he should be asked the same question, and gruffly answered, whereupon the gate was shut and they all passed along.

Then they came in sight of the palace of the Queen. What a sight that was! The walls were of pure coral, and all about the doors and windows were shells of every variety of colour and form. There were arches and pillars set around with shells, and in the corners grew graceful sea-weed, that clung to the palace and waved to and fro its long, soft leaves. Little Effie looked up and saw that the building was not finished, and that all around her there was a continual hum of movement. Then they entered the door of the palace and passed through long galleries, until they came to a great and beautiful door and heard within voices singing. A porter sat behind this door also, and asked the same questions, and they all answered as before, in one voice, only they spoke more softly. Now they stood in the great hall of the palace, and lo! there was the Queen herself, sitting on her throne, and about her were her maids of honour. It was they who had been singing, but who stopped when the procession came in. They were sitting at wheels and long stone looms, spinning and weaving wondrous robes of purple and scarlet and green; the Queen herself was weaving a gorgeous garment of all the most beautiful colours.

The little man stopped in front of the Queen and made three of his comical little bows, and all the attendant fishes bobbed their heads up and down; the dolphins gave some awkward, bungling shakes of the whole body that made the little fishes almost burst into laughing, and the old fellow with a sword looked exceedingly serious and made the most dignified bow imaginable. Then the Queen spoke:

"My faithful servant, hast thou obeyed my commands and brought the child of earth?"

"She is here, my good-loving Queen," said he. "What is thy will with her?" When little Effie heard this, she began to be frightened and to think—"Oh, dear! what is she going to do with me?" but the Queen looked so good that she felt at ease again and listened for what she would say.

"Take the child," said she, "and show her the beauties of my palace, and let her see the wonderful works that are done here; answer all her questions and bring her back to me again." Then they all bowed again. And as they moved away, Effie heard the song that the maidens at the wheels and looms sang.

The Song of the Sea-Maidens.

I.

Spin, maidens, spin! let the wheel go round!
Hours that once are lost can never more be found.
(*Chorus*) Work, hands! Love, heart!
Every one here has his part,——
Has his work to do,—has his love to give,
Thus we work, thus we love ever while we live.

II.

Weave, maidens, weave! let the shuttle fly!
Time and we are racing; faster, faster ply!
(*Chorus*) Work, hands! Love, heart! etc.

III.

Sing, maidens, sing! as ye spin and weave,
Work was never meant our joyous hearts to grieve,
(*Chorus*) Work, hands! Love, heart! etc.

IV.

As the wheel goes round—as the shuttle flies,
Let your songs and hearts upward, upward rise!
(*Chorus*) Work, hands! Love, heart!
Every one here has his part, etc.

They passed out of the hall, and the little sea green man said, "To the Top!" So they came to the top of the house, and there they saw hundreds and thousands of little coral insects, working to make the house more beautiful, and each, when he had done all that he could, lay down and died. And the little man told Effie how all this beautiful palace had been made by these insects and how it never would stop growing, but always some coral insect would be doing his tiny work, and when he had done all he could, would die.

"What is that humming?" asked Effie.

"That is the song they sing as they work," said he. "Listen! do you not hear it?" Effie listened hard and just caught a few words of the chorus.

"Every one here has his part——
Has his work to do, has his love to give,——
Thus we work, thus we love ever while we live."

"Why, that is what the maidens who were spinning sang," said she.

"Yes," said he, "they all sing the same song to different music." Then she began to hear the words all about her, and she found that the little sea green man, and the fishes, small and great, and the dolphins and the old constable sword fish were all singing the same song, each in his own way. So they went down again and through the whole palace and saw the shells, some of them indeed making pearls, but all singing the same song, and the sponges that were growing and the branches of coraline that one by one loosened themselves and floated upward, singing as they rose all about her, from corals and shells and grasses and sponges and fishes, came this one song, each singing it to his own air, yet the whole melody rising and sinking in a single harmonious strain.

Effie looked on at every thing in wonder, and at last they came back to the Queen's presence. She, too, was singing with her maidens; but when the procession came in again, and went through their bows once more, she said to the little sea-green man—and their voices were all hushed:

"My faithful servant, have you shown the little maiden all the wonders of the palace?"

"Yea, my good-loving Queen."

"And do they all spend their lives in good-working, singing as they work?"

"Yea, my good-loving Queen, all;" and the hum of the song rose all about her.

"Then back again lead the little child, and carry her to her home on earth, that she too may live and work and sing. For

Every one *there* has his part:
Has his work to do, has his love to give,"—

And all the voices sang with her

"Thus we work, thus we love ever while we live."

Then the procession moved out again, and Effie clung still to the little man's seal-skin cap, as she sat on her cushion of sea-weed, upon the hump on his back; and he marched along, using his flat hands like oars, while the gruff old constable with his sword, and the dolphins and the fishes, great and small, moved beside the pair, and they all went swiftly up from the light to the darker green, the voices growing fainter to Effie, and their forms more indistinct.

The little sea-green man brought Effie out of the water, and set her down on the beach, and then, making his profoundest bow, he walked off to the water again, the ends of his seal-skin cap dangling and bobbing behind. Effie watched him go under the water, and then walked up into the house. There was her mother frying some fish which Father Gilder had just brought home for supper, while he was chopping wood at the side of the house. It was not a bit like the beautiful palace she had seen, with the Queen of the Ocean Deeps, and her maidens about her, weav ing and singing songs. Effie wished the little sea-green man had never brought her up again, but had let her always live in such a beautiful place.

"What's the matter, Effie?" asked her mother, looking up from the frying-pan, and seeing Effie stand there, staring into the fire.

"Oh, mother!" said she, "I have seen such beautiful things!"

"Whereabouts, child!"

"Oh, way down under the water! Such a funny little man, all dressed in sea-weed, took me down on his back, and—"

"Nonsense, Effie! don't come to me with such stories. Go and wash your face and hands, and get yourself ready for supper."

"But really! mother,—"

"Sh! child; do as I tell you, and don't talk to *me* about your going down underneath the water; you'd ha' been wet through if you had."

"But he covered me all up with sea-weed."

"Poh! you've been asleep on the rock, and dreaming about it; it's a wonder you didn't fall off into the water. Come! run and wash yourself. Supper's most ready."

Effie went off pouting; and Mother Gilder took the frying-pan off the fire with the fish sizzling and smoking hot. "Come, father!" said she, "and Effie, hurry up! supper's on the table."

"Where's your little dog, Effie?" said her father. Effie didn't speak.

"Have you eat him up, eh?" Never a word from Effie.

"The child is naughty!" said her mother, "Effie, speak to your father!" But Effie looked crosser than ever.

"Well, you shall go to bed without your supper," said Mrs. Gilder, getting up, "if you're going to behave so. The little thing's been telling some ridiculous story about a man's taking her down under the water on his back!"

"He *did* take me down!" cried Effie, "and I wish I'd stayed there! erhn! erhn! erhn!" and she cried and cried.

"Soh, soh, little one," said Father Gilder, "you wouldn't want to leave your old father and mother, would you, Effie?"

"N-n-n-no, b-b-but m-m-mother said I didn't go."

"Ah, well! eat your supper, Effie, and then come and tell me all about it." So Effie ate her supper and then sat in her father's lap, and began to tell him all that I have told you; but before she had gone a great way, she was so sleepy that she couldn't tell any thing more, but kept saying, "And—and—and—a-n-d —a-n-d," till she fell fast asleep, and Mother Gilder put her to bed, and she did not wake up once more till the next morning.

"Well, what d'ye think, old man, about this stuff?" asked Mrs. Gilder, when Effie was snug in bed.

"Well, I don't know," said Mr. Gilder. "Its queer! its queer! I guess the child's been dreaming. Light my pipe, old woman."

So, when Mrs. Gilder had foraged in the pockets of her wonderful apron and brought out the tobacco and matches, and had filled the pipe and lighted it, the fisherman tilted his chair back against the chimney and smoked his pipe, and thought about it; but could not come to any conclusion, till at last his pipe went out, and he nodded, and nodded. Mother Gilder who sat on the other side of the fire-place, knitting a stocking that she brought out of one of her pockets, began to nod, too, waking up every once in a while to find she had dropped her stitches, and so making the needles go fast again for a few moments and then slower, till she nodded again, and at last she was fast asleep on one side of the fire-place, and Father Gilder on the other side, and little Effie in her crib. And we'll steal out on tip-toe, so as not to wake them, and come back again in just a year wanting one day.

Wish the Second.—On the Mountain.

ELL, we have been gone a year lacking one day, and here we are back again on the beach, and there is the cottage, and Mrs. Gilder by her table sewing on a frock for Effie, who is sitting on her seat—the great flat rock, you know— down by the water. Effie is a year older now, and this is her seventh birth-day. She has been a pretty good girl; but then she wished a great many times that she could have stayed at the bottom of the sea, and whenever she thought of it, she seemed to hear the song that they sang there. Now she was sitting on her seat, looking out for the old man, who you remember, had promised to come for her Second Wish. She had thought about him a good many times and had made up her mind what she would ask for. It was growing late and she began to be afraid he would not come. She thought she would walk down the beach and meet him; so she walked along looking for him all the while, when she spied a boat coming toward the shore; but she did not look at it much, she was so anxious to see her old man, and she thought she could make him out, just coming along in the distance. Pretty soon, the boat came up to the beach where she was, and a rough-looking sailor jumped out.

"Little girl," said he, "where does Simon Gilder live?"

"In that house, sir," pointing to the red cottage. "He is my father."

"So you're his little girl, are you? Is your father in the house?"

"No, sir, he is in the patch in the woods back there, hoeing potatoes."

"Will you go with me and show me where it is?" Effie looked along the beach and saw the old man, as she thought, slowly coming toward them; "Oh, dear!" thought she, "if the old man should come while I am gone!"

"What's the matter, little girl?" said the sailor-man when he saw she did not answer. "Are you afraid to go with me?"

"No," faltered Effie looking down. "But mother said I wasn't to go away from the beach."

"Oh, Effie, Effie!" said a voice close to her. She started. Why! that was the old man's voice; and when she looked up, there was no sailor-man and no boat, and no one coming down the beach; but the same old man that she saw last year, in the same grey clothes, with the same beautiful long white hair, and his

12

head shaking the same way as he bent down over his old smooth stick—the same old man stood by her.

"Oh, Effie!" said he in his beautiful voice, "you have deceived me. You weren't willing to do me a kindness; you cared too much about your own happiness. And this is your birth-day. I have come for your Second Wish. Remember, you have only one more wish after this. You must tell me this one before the sun goes down. Look!"

Effie looked as he pointed, and the sun stood just on the water's edge; and there were clouds above it and around it, but she thought it would go down clear. She had her wish all ready, though. "I wish," said she, "that I might go on to the great mountain off there," pointing back from the sea, "and see the birds and the trees and the flowers."

When she had said it, the clouds gathered before the sun, so that it could not be seen, and spread over the whole heavens, and she had hardly time to run to the cottage, before the rain began to pour down in torrents. Out at sea it was all black, except where the white caps of foam lighted up the waters; the waves rushed roaring on the beach, and the wind drove the sharp rain against the house. Effie put her face against the window-glass and peered out into the darkness, but she could see nothing of the old man.

"A bad ending to your birth-day, little Effie," said her father, coming in just then, all dripping wet. "Never mind. A bad beginning makes a good ending so your birth-day must have begun well, and this day is the beginning of the year for you, so the year'll end well. So it's good all round, ha! It's a bad night, wife! I hope nobody's out in the storm; it came up sudden."

Effie thought of the old man and shivered to think how wet and cold he would get. But she only thought of it a moment, and then began to wonder how the wish would come to pass, and whether another little sea-green man would come for her.

So she went to bed and to sleep. But, lo! before morning came she was waked by a tapping outside on the window-pane, close by her bed. At first she was frightened and put her head under the bed-clothes; then she thought, "Perhaps that is for me to go up on the mountain!" No sooner did she think of that than she heard the tapping again, and then a voice that said, "Come Effie! come with me to the mountain!"

Effie jumped out of bed and opened the window. The storm was over and the stars were shining brightly, while in the East was a patch of grey light, that showed the sun would rise before a great while. "Hurry! hurry!" said a voice near her, but she could not see anything. "Where are you?" said she. "Here," said the voice over her head. She looked up and there was a very indistinct white figure, that looked as if it might be a shadow. All she could see was something white like a robe, and two arms stretching out toward her; one of the hands came close to her; she caught hold of it, and in a moment was drawn up to the figure and wrapped in the white robe. Then a wind, blowing from the sea, bore them along and they flew off toward the mountains.

Now the mountains were a great way from the seashore, and Effie had never been there. She could see their tops from the house where she lived, and once in a while, somebody would come who had been there, and he would tell her about the trees and the brooks and the birds. Now she was to go there herself! She was held closely in the folds of the robe, only she could look out as she went and see the ground over which they were flying but they went so swiftly that she did not dare look down, so she looked up to the sky. The stars were growing fainter, and the long grey streak of dawn was growing brighter. They were nearing the mountain, too, and Effie could hear, once in a while, the tinkling of the brook as it rippled along below. At last they were close to the top of the mountain. There was a wide plain upon the top, covered with trees, while the springs of the brooks bubbled up there and flowed down the sides, and on the ground were flowers nestled among the leaves and the blades of grass.

"Look! and listen!" said the voice of the Figure that carried Effie, at the same time wheeling about, so that they faced the East. Effie looked. The stars were all gone now, save one in the distance—the morning-star. Everywhere overhead the sky was blue and clear—not a cloud to be seen; while away off before them in the East, the sky was tinged with deep, rich colours. Perfect quiet was everywhere. The wind was still; motionless the trees stood; on their boughs the birds sat, hardly rustling their feathers. She could just hear the tinkling of the brook. The flowers on the ground had their leaves folded, and near by a great eagle stood perched on a rock. The Figure holding Effie moved not at all, only as Effie sat breathless looking down to the ground, its hand pointed to the East and Effie again looked up there.

The sky was a fiery colour now, and far up toward the zenith, the crimson light shot its feathery rays; just above the horizon came a bit of gold; then higher it rose, till like a golden ball leaving the earth, it floated calmly up, up, soaring to heaven. The sun had risen! and the instant it lifted itself above the line, the voice of the figure said: "Listen!" and Effie listened. First she heard a low murmuring, and she saw the tops of the trees swaying back and forth, lifting their branches and bending them again toward the East; and as they murmured, the brooks struck in with their sparkling notes, and the trees and the brooks sang together; then the little birds on the branches opened their mouths, and their throats swelled, and out burst their pure sweet notes, chiming with the music of the trees and the brooks. Then the great, deep-mouthed wind came, first trembling and quavering, then with rich full breath, and the trees and the brooks, the birds and the wind, all sang the same glad song. The flowers opened their leaves and lifted their heads, the bright colours sparkling and shining; from the bushes sprang, fluttering, the gay butterflies and insects, and the large eagle spread its wings and sailed majestically in great circles toward the sun. Oh! it was a wonderful sight, and it was a wonderful song they sang! The whole mountain seemed to sing as the great golden sun rose higher and higher.

Only Effie was silent. Then the Figure wrapped her closer, and turning, flew back toward the seashore. "What was the song they sang?" asked Effie. "I could not tell the words." "You could not tell the words," said the voice of the Figure, "because you did not sing with them. If you had sung with them, you would have heard the words. I can only tell you a little of it, but if you sing these words, the rest will some time come to you. They all sang at the first —

"Praise to Thee! Praise to Thee!
Thou art all Purity.
Thou art the Source of Light—
Scatter Thou the dark night.
Shine on us! shine on us!"

Effie said the words over, and the voice said again "If you sing them with the song of the sea-maidens you will understand them better." Then Effie fell asleep, just as they came again to the open window and she knew nothing more till she was waked by her mother calling out—

"Effie, child! wake up! the sun was up long ago! come! come!"

Effie started up. It was broad daylight. Her father was out-doors, looking after his nets, and her mother was getting the table ready for breakfast. She dressed herself quickly, saying over in mind the words just taught her. Then she recollected that she could understand them better if she sang the song of the sea. So she said that to herself also.

"Do you go and get some water to put in the kettle, Effie," said her mother.

"Yes, mother," said she, and as she went she sang to herself—

"Work, hands! Love, heart!
Every one here has his part."

"Good-morning, little one," said her father, meeting her in the door-way; "here's a bright day for your new year!"

"Isn't it!" said Effie, giving him a kiss and then singing—

"Praise to thee! Praise to thee;
Thou art all Purity.
Thou art the Source of Light."

"I believe the child's going to be a good girl, wife," said Father Gilder, coming into the house.

"Well, I hope she is, for she's been sulky enough before this," said Mother Gilder.

"True, true," replied he, "but sulky birds don't sing."

The year went slowly by. Effie sang the two songs as she worked, and helped her mother and was a com fort to her father. Every morning when she got up, she sang the Song of the Mountain, and through the day she kept singing, too, the Song of the Sea. Very often she thought of the old man, and wondered what she should ask for the third and last time he came. She thought she ought to ask for the best thing she could think of, but for a long time she could not make up her mind, until a few days before her birth-day, as she was singing the two songs. Then was she impatient for the day to come, that she might ask her last and great wish.

Wish the Third.—In the Cottage.

THE eighth birth-day came at last, but before the sun was to set, Mrs. Gilder called her. "Here, Effie," said she, "I want you to go down cellar before it is dark, and sweep it clean. It's dreadfully dirty."

"Must I go now, mother?"

"Yes, right off; it'll be too dark if you don't make haste," and Mrs. Gilder drew a bunch of keys out of one of her apron pockets and unlocked the closet door and brought out a broom for Effie. Effie took the broom and went down cellar. "Well," thought she, "I must do my work at any rate, and the old man may not come by till I get it done." So she set to work, sweeping out the cellar. She had just finished and stooped to pick up a perverse chip. As she lifted herself up, there stood that same old man again!

"Why! how *did* you get in, sir?" said she.

"The sun is most down, Effie," said he without answering her question, "what is your Last Wish?" As he said it his head shook harder than ever before, and he leaned on his cane so that he was almost bent double.

"Oh, sir! I wish," said Effie, "that I might do some great work that should make others happy, and that I might be able to sing the whole of the Song of the Mountain." As she said this the old man raised his head slowly from his staff, and when she finished, lo! he was changed into a great beam of light that cast its rays all about the cellar. Effie flew up stairs with her broom, and ran to the cottage door. The sea was sparkling with light, and the sun went down clear and beautiful.

"Aye! there's a sunset for you, chicky," said Father Gilder, coming up from the shore. "There'll be no storm after that! Do you remember your last birth day, little one, when there was such a sudden storm came up?" Yes, indeed, Effie remembered it and wondered whether the sky would always be clear now.

The next day Effie looked for somebody to come and give her some great thing to do, and teach her the Song of the Mountain, as she had wished for her last wish. But no one came—no, nor the next day, nor the day after; and then every thing went wrong. Her mother became sick and cross, and finally died; and Effie had to wear the wonderful apron with so many pockets, and work hard every day. How could she do any great work? All she could do was to take care of the house and do little things—ever so many of them there were, too, so that when the evening came she was quite tired out. But her father said she was a comfort to him, and he loved to have her sit by him and sing to him. She sang the two songs over and over, as she did every day at her work, and never tired of singing them, nor did he tire of hearing them.

So she lived on. She had a great many more birthdays, but no old man came to see her, and nobody came to give her a great work to do, or to teach her the rest of the song. By and by her father died too, but Effie lived still in the little red cottage by the sea-shore. And if any were sick or in trouble, they were sure to come to her. For every body loved her, and wherever she went she seemed to carry the sunlight with her, and to make everybody better and happier. Still no one came, though every birth-day she sat at the door, looking for the old man.

But he did come at last. It was her birth-day. She was an old woman, but she sat in the door-way as she used to, watching for somebody to come to her with a great work to do, and the rest of the song. She sat in her great arm-chair, and her eyes were very dim so that she could not see very well, and her ears were very dull, so that she could hardly hear at all. There was the sun that had so often gone down without any one's appearing. But before it touched the water she heard a voice—that old sweet voice that she had never forgotten, saying, "Effie!" She looked, and there she saw the same face that the old man used to have, but that was all she could see. Then it said again, "Effie!" and she said:

"Oh, sir! have you come at last to give me my wish? I have looked for you year after year, and now I am an old woman, and have not many more days to live."

"Your wish has been granted, Effie. You asked for some great work to do to make others happy. All your life since you have been doing the great work. There is nothing right or holy done for others that is not great. The little daily duties that you did so faithfully; the little kindnesses you showed to others; the little pleasant words you spoke—these are all great things."

"But the Song of the Mountain?" asked Effie.

"Dear child," said he, "you have sung the song all your life. If you have thanked God for his goodness to you—if you have loved him for his love to you—if you have prayed to him to make you good and holy—you have sung the Song of the Mountain."

"Praise to thee! Praise to thee!" murmured the old woman. Then she thought she heard the whole mountain singing as it did the morning she listened to it; and the great song was sung, and she sang also, and the voice beside her sang.

——The people who lived about there say, that when they came in the morning to see Old Effie, she was sitting in her arm-chair, with her hands folded, and her lips half parted as if she had sung herself to sleep; and when they touched her she did not move—for Old Effie was dead.

A Christmas Stocking
With a Hole in it

I.
The Stocking is Hung.

AT Christmas-tide in New York, the people who live in the upper part of the city cannot hear the chimes that ring from Trinity steeple; but in the dwelling streets which run in and out among the warehouse streets, and in the courts which stand stock still and refuse to go a step further,—there the Trinity music is heard and the "merry Christmas" of the bells is flung out to all however poor. Beside Trinity there are but few chimes of bells in the city, neither do poor children there sing Christmas carols in the streets and thus unlatch the doors of even crabbed hearts.

But the merriest chimes of bells are played and the sweetest carols sung even in New York. For when at Christmas one walks in the crowded streets he may hear on all sides the merry Christmas! merry Christmas to you! to you! rung out on every key and the chiming makes perfect music; the poor children sing carols too, for are they not each little songs as they stand in their rags before well-to-do folk—songs without words—reminding us of the poor child Jesus and the blessings which He brought? Yes, the bells ring in our hearts and we hear carols then at least if not at other times; and in some old cobwebbed heart does Christmas fancy or Christmas memory enter and ring disused bells that sound but a hoarse blessing, so rusty has their metal become, but a blessing at least well-meant. Blessed be Christmas that it knocks so at the door of our hearts.

Now it was on a certain Christmas that some very pleasant chimes were rung, and that too within hearing of Trinity bells. In the street on Christmas eve were Bundles of great coats and furs tied together with tippets, who hurried along like locomotives, puffing and snorting and leaving behind a line of smoke. But all the people in the streets were not Bundles, by any means. Some scarcely had any wrappings, let alone such heavy coverings as great coats and furs. Little boys may be Bundles if they are properly wrapped up and tied with a tippet or scarf, but not all little boys are Bundles. On this eve one might see many who were not. They kept their hands in their pockets or breathed upon their red fingers, and drew their shoulders together and screwed their faces as if they were trying to hide behind themselves, while the wind blew through every crevice of their bodies and rattled the teeth in their mouths.

One of these little boys upon this very Christmas eve hung up his stocking, and what became of it is now to be told. His name was Peter Mit. He had been out all day selling cigars, and was on his way home to supper. But hungry and cold as he was, he could not help stopping to look through the shop-windows at the beautiful things spread out so temptingly behind them. Such toys and games and picture books! "Now," said he, "I must run;" but just as he started, he came to a window so much finer than any he had seen that he stopped before this also. There was a string fastened across the inside of the window with picture and story papers hung upon it; the glass was not very clear, for the frost made it almost like crown-glass, but it was clear enough in the corner to shew one of the pictures, which was a double one; in one part there was a little boy in his night-gown hanging a stocking upon the door of his bed-chamber; in the other part the little boy is shown snugly asleep in his bed, while a most odd little man hung over with toys and picture books of all kinds stands on tip-toe before the stocking, filling it with playthings. There was some printing underneath that explained the picture; as well as Peter could make out, this little boy like a great many others hung up his stocking before he went to bed on Christmas eve, and some time during the night, Santa Klaus, a queer old man, very fond of little folk, came down the chimney and filled the stocking with presents. This was all new to little Peter, and astonished him exceedingly; but it was really too cold to stand there looking at even the most wonderful picture, so he blew into his red fist, and ran off home, taking long slides on the ice wherever he could.

He left the bright Main Street and turning one or two corners came to Fountain Court. That is a fine-sounding name, but the houses are very wretched and low, though quite grand people lived there in olden times; where the fountain was no one could say, unless the wheezy pump that stands at the head of the court were meant for it; of this the Pump itself had no doubt. It was very large and had a long heavy handle that always stood out stiffly; there was a knob on the top of the pump that had once been gilded but that was a long time ago, when the Pump was aristocratic and presumed itself to be a Fountain. It was dingy and broken now, but the Pump was none the less proud and dignified; it took pleasure in holding out its handle stiffly and never letting it down though people stumbled against it every day. "It had been there the longest," the Pump said, "it had a right to the way; people must learn to turn out for it."

It was down this Fountain Court—though people now generally called it Pump Court—that little Peter Mit ran as fast as his legs could carry him. He stopped at the fourth house on the right-hand side; it was a low building, only a story and a half high, yet a respectable merchant had lived there formerly. Before the door stood a battered wooden image of a savage Indian, holding out a bunch of cigars in his hand, and looking as if he meant to tomahawk you if you didn't take one. The Indian was quite stuck over with snow-balls, for he was a fine mark for the boys in the court, who divided their attention between his head and the knob on top of the Pump. If it were not so dark, one might spell out on the dingy sign over the door, the names "MORGRIDGE AND MIT DEALERS IN TOBACCO." The only window was adorned with half a dozen boxes of cigars, a few pipes, a bottle of snuff, and a melancholy plaister sailor, who had been smoking one pipe, with his hands in his pockets, as long as the oldest inhabitant in the court could remember.

Peter Mit opened the door from the street and entered the shop; one solitary oil lamp stood upon the counter, behind which sat David Morgridge, the surviving partner of the firm of Morgridge and Mit Dealers in Tobacco. Solomon Mit, the uncle of little Peter had been dead five years, and on dying had bequeathed his orphan-nephew to his partner, and so as Mr. Morgridge had no children, and Peter had no father, the two lived together alone in the old house.

Mr. Morgridge was not a talkative man—one would see that at a glance; his mouth looked as if it shut with a spring. Mr. Mit, when living had been even more silent, but when he did speak—then one would look for golden words; for so small a man he was surely very wise. Mr. Morgridge used to say that it was because his name was Solomon, and that was the only thing Mr. Morgridge had ever said that came near being witty. All the court knew it, and the saying almost turned the corner at the head of the court. They divided the business between them Mr. Morgridge attending to the snuff department, Mr. Mit to the cigar and pipe branch. It was the intention of Mr. Mit, expressed soon after the adoption of little Peter, to bring him up to take charge of the chewing tobacco branch. In consequence of this division of the business, David Morgridge took snuff incessantly, but never smoked. Solomon Mit smoked all the while but never took snuff. They did this to recommend their wares. Besides, it served to explain the duty of each partner. If a customer came in for pipes or cigars he invariably went directly to Mr. Mit; if he came for snuff, he as surely turned to Mr. Morgridge.

When Peter entered the shop, Mr. Morgridge was just wiping his face after a pinch of snuff; the whole air of the shop was snuffy, and no one came in without instantly being tempted to sneeze. Peter sneezed as a matter of course, and Mr. Morgridge, after his usual fashion, replied with a "God bless you!" He seldom got the compliment in return, however, as in his case the blessing would have become so common as to be quite worthless. Mr. Morgridge then in quired into Peter's sales, and with that his regular conversation ended. His mouth shut so closely, with the corners turned down to cover any possible opening, that one would know immediately that no accidental words could escape. But to-night Peter did not mean to let his guardian keep his usual silence; he was too much concerned about the picture he had seen in the shop-window. He waited however till after tea. Then, as they returned to the shop, Mr. Morgridge taking his customary seat upon his bench, with a pot of snuff beside him, set about his work of putting up tobacco in divers shapes. Peter took his customary seat also, much above Mr. Morgridge. It was a seat which he had inherited from his uncle. Solomon Mit, being a contemplative man, was desirous of being lifted above ordinary things when he pursued his meditations, and had accordingly built a sort of watch-tower out of several boxes, placed one upon another, and topped by an arm-chair, deprived of its legs. Into this chair Solomon used to climb, and when there, his head was not far from the ceiling. Here he would sit in his lofty station, and wrapped in the smoke from his own pipe, would revolve in his mind various questions, occasionally dropping from the clouds a remark to his partner, who sat snuffing below on the bench. Customers, when they entered the shop, had become used to the sight of the little man's legs as they appeared below the cloud, and a classical scholar chancing in one day to fill his pipe, had likened him to Zeus upon the top of Olympus.

Peter valued this watch-tower above all his possessions, and here every night he sat perched, and counted the fly-specks on the ceiling, or fished up things from the floor by means of a hook and line which he kept by him. To-night, however, after he had climbed into the chair, he broke the usual silence by putting the following question to Mr. Morgridge:

"Mr. Morgridge, is this Christmas Eve?" to which David Morgridge, after taking a pinch of snuff cautiously replied:

"It may be;" and then added, as if to explain his uncertainty of mind—"I don't keep the run o' Christmas."

"Does Santa Klaus really come down a chimney Christmas night and fill the stocking with presents?" proceeded Peter. And then, getting no answer, he gave an account of what he had seen in the window, and being very much interested, he told also what he thought of it all, and the resolution that he had finally come to, namely, to hang up his own stocking that very night. Mr. Morgridge having listened to what Peter had to say, took more snuff and seemed disposed to let that end the matter, but Peter persisted in getting his opinion.

"Mr. Morgridge," said he, "do you think Santa Klaus will come and fill my stocking?" Being pressed for an answer, Mr. Morgridge made shift to say—

"May be, but should say not; used to believe in Santa Klaus when I was a boy; don't now; 'taint no use."

This was rather discouraging, but Peter upon thinking it over on his watch-tower, reflected that Mr. Morgridge used to believe in Santa Klaus, and that the queer fellow only visited boys: besides, he thought it might be owing to the snuff that he disbelieved in him now; for it was by that Peter usually explained Mr. Morgridge's eccentricities.

But Peter was tired and drowsy, and clambering down from his perch, set out for his bed, groping his way up the steep staircase that led to the half-story above, where he had his cot. He never went up that staircase in the dark—and a light was a luxury not to be thought of—without imagining all manner of horrors which he might see at the top. In one place, there were two small holes in the floor close together; the place was over the shop, and whenever there was a light burning below, he could see these two holes blinking and shining like two eyes. It was the last thing he saw when he got into bed, and he would say to himself in a bold way, as if to show any ghosts or goblins that might possibly be about, how undaunted he was, "Two Eyes! come here and swallow me up!" and then he would draw the bed-clothes over his head for a minute or two, and peep out to reassure himself that Two Eyes had not taken him at his word and come to swallow him up. But Two Eyes never came, and this gave him fresh courage, so that of late he had become quite bold in the dark.

As he climbed up the staircase this night, his little head was full of the idea of Santa Klaus. The chimney was convenient, he thought to himself, for it passed through the loft and there was a large open fire-place in it never used. But then, suppose he should come down before the fire in the room below was fairly out! he would get scorched. But it was too cold to sit long guessing about such matters, so he undressed himself quickly. Last of all, he drew off his right stocking. This he held in his hand—"Oh!" said he, "it has got a hole in it; the things will all come out!" Indeed, it was almost all hole, for beside the proper hole which every stocking has or it isn't a stocking, there was a hole in the heel and another very large one in the toes. He looked at it in despair, and then took up the other one; but that was even worse. He consoled himself, finally, as well as he could, by the reflection that Santa Klaus would probably put all the large things in first, and thus they would stop the holes up and nothing would be lost.

He cast about now for a place to hang it. The little boy in the picture hung his on the door, but that was out of the question, for there was no nail there. He remembered finally a hook in the wall not far from the chimney. It was a dreadful place to go to, so near Two Eyes! but he mustered courage, especially when he considered how very convenient it would be for Santa Klaus. His heart went pit-a-pat as he stole over the floor; the boards under his feet creaked and every bone in his body seemed to be going off like a firecracker.

It seemed to him as if Two Eyes and all his friends were starting from every corner of the room.

Going back was not so bad as all the ghosts were now behind him. He shivered into his cold bed, and drew his knees up to his chin. So excited was he about Santa Klaus, that when he looked presently toward the other end of the room and saw Two Eyes blinking at him, he forgot for the instant that he had ever seen them before, and fancied Santa Klaus must have made his appearance already. He was just ready to scream, when he recollected what the Eyes were, and boldly saying:—

"Two Eyes! come here and swallow me up!" he rolled himself up in the bed clothes and was soon fast asleep.

II.
Midnight.

THE clock of Trinity struck twelve. One would have thought from the long pause after each stroke, that it had great difficulty in making out the complete number. Really it was so long about it because it wished to give plenty of time for starting to the various persons and things in the neighborhood, who are wont to be agog at that hour only. The Man on St. Paul's, however, was so long getting ready that the twelfth stroke came before he was fairly off,—so he lost his chance for this time. It is so with him every night. When the first stroke comes it startles him and he rubs his eyes and wonders where he is; he continues to rub his eyes and wonder till the sixth stroke has sounded. Then he collects his thoughts a little, and by the ninth stroke remembers that if he is quick enough, he can shut up his book, get down from his high and uncomfortable perch, and stretch his legs a little in a ramble through the church-yard or round the Park. Having to be in a hurry, for it must be done during the three following strokes, he gets confused, and before he can muster sufficient presence of mind, the clock has struck twelve, and he must wait another day.

The Grocer on the City Hall was in a difficult predicament. It has long been his intention to get down with his scales and weigh the City Corporation. He tries to do it when the clock strikes twelve, as that is his only chance. He heard the first stroke, and was on the alert. He indeed succeeded in reaching the ground, but he could not find the Corporation, though he searched the Hall and the Park. All that he could discover was a sleepy alderman. He returned to his place in disgust. He could not see, for his part, why the Corporation did not sit in the night-time; it would seem to be the proper hour. This he said to the

23

Eagle perched on a pole near by, and who had just returned from a visit to his grand-uncle who has been all his life on the point of dropping an umbrella, point downward, on the greatest rogue in the city. The Eagle found his grand-uncle had not yet dropped the umbrella, because he was not sure that he had found the greatest rogue.

But other people and things are not so stupid as the Man on St. Paul's, nor so unsuccessful as the Grocer. They are brisker and seize the opportunity to enjoy themselves. The Pump, for instance, that stands at the head of Fountain Court, generally indulges himself in a soliloquy. He talks through his nose, to be sure, which sounds disagreeably, but the nearest listeners do not mind it. For the Man on St. Paul's is too stupid or it may be asleep. The Grocer is running round with his scales, looking for the Corporation. Sir Walter Raleigh has taken so much snuff that his own voice is even more disagreeable, and so he has no right to complain. The nearest listener of all would be the Indian in front of Morgridge and Mit, dealers in tobacco, but he has gone to have a talk with Sir Walter Raleigh; so the Pump has it all its own way. Let us hear what the Pump said this night:—

"Well, so it's Christmas again, is it? how the years do go by! and how things change! To think of the difference between this court now and what it used to be! Why, I can remember very well when fine ladies and gentlemen gathered here on Christmas eve. The watchman would go along with them with a lantern in his hand. I was of importance then—I am now, to be sure, but then people recognized me and considered me. I gave the name to the court—that was something! But those days went by; and then there was that time when a noisy fellow got up on my head, where he kept his place with difficulty, and spouted ever so much eloquence about rights and liberty and constitution. No good ever came of that! for it was he who broke off a piece of the gilt knob on my head, and it has never been mended since. That was the beginning of my troubles, and now to what a pass have things come. Why, a ragged, drunken man leaned up against me—ugh! this very night, and I see the poorest kind of people go down the court. I was used to have nothing but fine pitchers and pails brought to me to fill, but now I have to look into dirty broken pitchers and old tubs. They have even begun to call the place Pump Court, as if I were no better than a common every-day pump! What is worst, there is an upstart just the other side of the way,—it lets out water to be sure, but it has nothing to say about it; it has no handle, and the water comes out by just turning a screw; altogether it is a very plebeian thing; it can know nothing of the pleasure of feeling a box go rumbling down your inside, and fetching up water from the depths of the earth.

"There go the Christmas bells! Many a time I've heard them before and seen Santa Klaus hurrying along to visit every house in the court. He never goes near them now, and no wonder, for he can't care to associate with such low people. When he does come, he looks soberer, and not so jolly as he used to;

nor does he bring so many and such fine things. I am in fact the only respectable thing in the neighborhood. But bless my boxes! what a shock that was! somebody must have struck my handle; served him right; he ought to turn out. I've been here the longest."

It was the sleepy alderman who was hastening by. "Confound that pump-handle!" said he. "That's the second time to-day I've stumbled against it. I'll have the pump taken up and carted off to-morrow. It's a nuisance; nobody wants it here."

It was difficult to make out what the Pump said to this; it was so choked with rage at the indignity, that only a confused gurgling could be distinguished in its throat. But that was the end of its soliloquy.

The Pump was partly right. Santa Klaus did not visit the court as often as he used, nor did he bring such fine presents with him. But it was not because he disliked the society that he did not come, it was because they did not hang stockings up. The stocking must be hung or he will not go—that is the rule. He is wonderfully keen in scent; he will go straight to a stocking even if it be hidden in the darkest corner. He cares nothing about time or place either. He can be where he chooses at any moment. So, just as the twelfth stroke of Trinity sounded, Santa Klaus was in Fountain Court. The Indian was scurrying down the place with his cigars in his hand, and taking his stand before Morgridge and Mit, put on his face its fiercest expression as the sound of the stroke died away. At the same moment Santa Klaus was in the house, in the loft where little Peter Mit had hung his stocking. Whether he entered by the chimney or not, it is impossible to say, but I suspect he did, for the door was locked and there was no other entrance.

At any rate there he was, and standing on tip-toe by Peter's stocking. He began to fill it and emptied one of his pockets. "Really," said he, "this is a very capacious stocking." It was not full yet, and he emptied into it another pocketful. "This is remarkable!" said he, stopping in amazement, "it is as roomy as a meal-bag. What an extraordinary foot that little boy must have!"

Santa Klaus' clothes are all pocket pretty much, and he emptied the contents of a third into the stocking, which was still not full. Then he stopped to examine it. "Oh! oh!" said he, "this is very bad! there is a hole in the stocking!" It would never do to keep pouring things in at one end while they passed out at the other, and his presents could only be placed in stockings. So Santa Klaus sorrowfully gathered up the presents, and leaving the stocking as empty as he found it, was off in a twinkling.

III.

25

THE moment Santa Klaus whisked out of the room, Kleiner Traum whisked in. It is impossible to say how he got into the room either; it is enough that he was there. Kleiner Traum is a very remarkable personage. He is like Santa Klaus in this, that he moves very quickly and can make visits in one night all over the world. But more than that, he has the power of making people see just what he chooses. Some persons think that they have seen two Kleiner Traums, a good and a bad, but the fault is in their eyes. He carries a kaleidoscope with him and shakes it before people; just how he shakes it, so are the things they see. These things are very apt to be like what has happened to them at different times, only much more grotesque.

Kleiner Traum had come to make Peter Mit a visit, and show him his kaleidoscope. Little Peter was fast asleep—that is the only time when Kleiner Traum visits people,—and snugly curled up in bed. He was not thinking or dreaming about anything, when now Kleiner Traum held the kaleidoscope before him, and gave it a twist. What now did he see?

He saw an exceedingly queer-looking man squeeze out of the fire-place; he was hung over with toys, and his pockets bulged out with the things inside; in fact, he was quite the image of the little man he had seen in the picture in the shop-window, and Peter made up his mind instantly that it was Santa Klaus. As soon as he got on his legs in the middle of the room, Two Eyes, whom Peter had so often called upon to swallow him up, began moving about, apparently trying to mislead Santa Klaus. Peter was ready to scream out, but for the life of him he couldn't make a sound. He watched Two Eyes, who seemed to think he would draw Santa Klaus to the head of the staircase, and then dance about so as to make him tumble headlong down the steps. But Santa Klaus was too knowing for Two Eyes. Peter saw him go to the door as if expecting to find the stocking there, and then not finding it, turn about and walk around the room till he came to where it hung upon the hook.

Peter was now terribly excited, and Kleiner Traum gave the kaleidoscope another twist. During the process of twisting, Peter's mind was in a queer jumble, and he thought he saw Two Eyes peeping out of the stocking, and Santa Klaus sitting on the Pump at the head of the court; but as soon as the kaleidoscope was still, it was clear again, and he could see Santa Klaus standing on tip-toe before the stocking and emptying into it the contents of his pockets.

The first thing he took out was a tin trumpet; just such a one as Peter had himself seen in a shop-window the day before. This he put into the stocking, giving a chuckle and trying it to see if it were good; it sounded splendidly. Then came a sled. It was astonishing how it ever came out of Santa Klaus' pocket and still more astonishing how it could get into the stocking. Yet surely

Peter saw it enter, and that very easily. After the sled came a monkey-jack. Before he put it in Santa Klaus twitched the monkey, and made it turn summersaults over the stick, till he was nearly ready to fall down with laughing at it. A mask came next—a leering mask with a long nose, and eyes, frightful enough to scare all the people in the court. Then followed a warm muffler for the head; it was a very comfortable looking thing. No sooner was the muffler safely in than a pint of peanuts rolled into the stocking, and after the peanuts came some marbles, and after the marbles, a dozen red apples, and after the apples a pair of skates, and after the skates a bundle of candy.

It certainly was astonishing to see how much the stocking would hold. Peter could hardly believe his eyes, yet there it was, and he saw everything that went into it. But the candy was the last thing; the stocking was now full and the candy peeped out at the top. Peter saw Santa Klaus look approvingly at the stocking, give it a pat and disappear through the fire-place again, looking just as full of presents as when he came down.

At this point Kleiner Traum turned the kaleidoscope, and Peter was all in a jumble again. Apparently the stocking was going up the chimney and Santa Klaus was riding on the toe, while Two Eyes was coming toward Peter to swallow him up. Peter was just on the point of giving himself up for lost, expecting the next moment to be swallowed up by Two Eyes, when it was clear again, and Two Eyes was in his old place, and the stocking was hanging on its hook; only Santa Klaus had disappeared up the chimney. For you see, Kleiner Traum's kaleidoscope was quiet again.

Now what did Peter see? The stocking was swollen to an enormous bulk, and what was more, Peter could see everything that was going on inside. He saw that they were quarrelling about the places they should occupy; for in the heel and in the toe of the stocking, were the two holes which were now of an alarming size. The Sled commenced the trouble. It felt itself slowly but surely slipping toward the hole in the toe, with the weight of all the other things on him. "Don't crowd so!" Peter heard the Sled say to the Tin Trumpet.

"I'm not pushing," said the Tin Trumpet; "I'd give anything if I weren't sliding so toward that dreadful hole!" "Monkey-Jack, I'll thank you to keep that stick of yours out of my mouth." Just then, an apple losing its footing, dropped through the hole in the heel of the stocking, and Peter heard it go rolling over the floor; another quickly followed, and another.

"Oh!" said the Mask, "this is getting dangerous; there is a dreadful cavity under me; but I'll put a bold face on it. There goes another apple." Peter heard apple follow apple out of the hole in the heel, till the whole dozen were on the floor, where they still went rolling off after each other toward the staircase when they hopped thumpty-thump down the steps, till the last one had gone. Meanwhile the Sled, the Tin Trumpet and the Monkey-Jack were having a sad time in the foot of the stocking. "I cannot hold on much longer," said the Sled, and it had hardly spoken the words, before it slid out through the toe, and Peter heard it go sliding over the floor and follow the apples down the staircase.

Matters were no better, but rather worse in the leg of the stocking. A weak voice was heard in the corner. It was a Peanut complaining bitterly of the Marbles. "If ye had not come in here among us," it said, "we should have done very well, but now ye are pushing us all toward the hole." The Marbles could not reply, they were too frightened themselves; they had crowded in among the Peanuts for safety, and now there was danger of both going. One large Marble alone held them all back; it was wedged in by the Monkey-Jack, and the Monkey-Jack had its stick in the Tin Trumpet's mouth. But the Tin Trumpet had only caught by a single thread of the stocking; that gave way, and down came the Trumpet followed by the Monkey-Jack. The Trumpet rolled off toward the door like the rest, and the Monkey-Jack went head-over-heels after it. Of course the large Marble had no help for it now; he dropped out of the heel, and the rest of the Marbles came tumbling after with the Peanuts in the midst of them. The Marbles and Peanuts, unlike the rest, rolled off toward Two Eyes; the Marbles disappeared through one eye, the Peanuts through the other.

It seemed of no avail now for the rest to keep their place. "It is no use to keep up appearances longer," said the Mask, and he dropped out and walked off on his nose. The Skates who had not spoken before, now turned to the Muffler and said: "We shall cut a pretty figure going through the hole like the rest, we may not go after all; there's many a slip—" but before they had finished the sentence they had followed the rest, and were striking out for the door.

Nothing now remained but the Muffler and the Candy. The Muffler spoke in a thick voice, "I am a sort of relation to the stocking and intend to remain by it, if it is a poor relation. It won't turn me out of doors, surely." The Candy, replied in a sweet voice, "As for me, I shall stick to the stocking. My dear Muffler, you quite melt me, you are so warm and affectionate."

After this point, Peter could see or hear nothing further, and for a very good reason—Kleiner Traum had vanished with his kaleidoscope.

IV.
Kleiner Traum Visits David Morgridge.

T is no secret whither Kleiner Traum vanished. The moment he had left little

Peter Mit, he was sitting on David Morgridge's breast, kaleidoscope in hand.

One shake of the kaleidoscope. Really, Mr. Morgridge sees strange things. He sees a little boy no bigger than Peter Mit, in a snug little room, hanging up on the door a red and white plaid stocking. The strangest thing is that he remembers the place and surroundings perfectly. He knows the cozy room, the white dimity curtains, the little cot bed, the sixteen-paned window looking out on the church-spire and the meadow; it was as if he had skipped sixty years of his life backward, for the little boy was a diminutive David Morgridge.

But the kaleidoscope makes quick shifts. Here is another turn, and Mr. Morgridge, as if he were a picture on the wall, is looking at a room which he knows well enough. It is the tobacco shop. There are two men in it; one sits on the bench and takes snuff, and does up little paper pellets; the other is just discoverable under a cloud of tobacco smoke, perched upon the top of a small observatory. This, too, is Christmas Eve, for so the little man on the watch-tower announces, as if he kept the calendar of the seasons, and piped an "All's Well" to his comrade below.

"David," he says, "David Morgridge! This is Christmas Eve. 'On earth peace, good will toward men.' That's what the Bible says, and that's what Trinity chimes say. How many Christmases have we kept together? eighteen, David; then that's eighteen turkeys for the poor folk, though bless us we're not much richer." This is a long speech for Solomon Mit, yet the man snuffing on the bench says nothing, but scowls. Then does Solomon Mit clamber down from his watch-tower, and with his cheery, piping voice sing a Christmas hymn, and though David Morgridge never lends his voice, the little man is no whit disheartened, but ends with laying his hand on David's shoulder and heartily wishing—"God bless you, David Morgridge, old friend—God bless us all!" and climbs once more to the top of his tower.

Quickly turns the kaleidoscope again, and now Mr. Morgridge, like a shadow in the dark that can see but not be seen, is in the room where he is now sleeping. But he is not on the bed, he is standing by the side of it, and the old cheery voice, though weaker now, of Solomon Mit comes from the pillow. The little man has come down from his tower for the last time, and has puffed his last pipeful of tobacco smoke. This, too, is Christmas Eve, and Solomon Mit has not forgotten it. Listen, he is speaking now.

"David Morgridge, old friend, twenty years we've lived together. You've been a true friend to me. We haven't said much, but we've trusted each other. I'm the first to go, and I'm glad to go on Christmas Eve. I'd like to go when the bells are ringing and Trinity is chiming, 'Peace on earth, good will toward men;' that's it David. Don't forget the turkeys; twenty you know; and don't make 'em chickens. You haven't always liked to give them, but you will now. And you'll be good to little Peter. I bequeath him to you, David, to hold and to keep in trust; and all that's mine in the shop; it's all yours. There are the bells—

"'All glory be to God on high,
And to the Earth be peace'"—

But Solomon Mit has sung without finishing his last hymn.

What more Mr. Morgridge might have seen, we shall never know, for at this point Kleiner Traum and his kaleidoscope vanished, and did not come back that night at any rate.

V.

Morgridge Klaus.

WHEN does Christmas Day begin? It can never be determined, but most people think it begins when they wake, though all do not wake at once; the children generally have the longest Christmas Day. Now, in Fountain Court, almost before daylight, there was some one astir. He came out of the door of Morgridge & Mit, dealers in tobacco, and toddled up the court at an astonishing gait. Where did he go to? he certainly passed the pump and turned the corner, and in a quarter of an hour more was trotting down the court with a parcel in his hand. The door of Morgridge & Mit closes behind him, but not before we have seen his face. Verily, it is Mr. Morgridge, but so extraordinarily like Santa Klaus is he, that we are puzzled to know which of the two it is; the form and shoulders are those of Mr. Morgridge, but the face at least is borrowed from Santa Klaus; Mr. Morgridge never in his life looked so jolly. Not to confound this person with the sour-faced man who sat glumpy, upon the bench taking snuff, the night before, let us call him Morgridge Klaus.

Morgridge Klaus stole slily up stairs to Peter Mit's loft. He went up stairs because there was so much of the Morgridge about him; if there had been more of the Klaus he would undoubtedly have come down the chimney. At the top of the stairs, where it was still quite dark, he could see Peter curled up in bed. But it was not he that he had come to see. He began groping about on the floor in search of something. "Ah! here it is!" he said with a chuck le, bringing to light a stocking most woefully riddled with holes. Morgridge Klaus stuffed a paper parcel into the stocking, and laying it carefully on the floor, stumbled down stairs, chuckling to himself and taking snuff immoderately.

Mr. Morgridge's Christmas Day had in fact commenced, but it was an hour yet before Peter Mit began his Christmas Day. The little fellow rubbed his eyes and drew his knees nearer his chin when he awoke. Then he remembered the day and looked eagerly toward the chimney. There hung his stocking, as small,

30

as full of holes, and as empty as when he hung it. "So it was a dream only after all," he said sorrowfully. Still he went over to it in hopes that the dream might have come true, and that the candy and muffler had remained by the stocking, but they too were gone. Peter shiveringly dressed himself. He had now only one stocking and a shoe to put on. How heavy the stocking was! there was something in it! Peter grew greatly excited—"Santa Klaus must have taken this stocking after all!" said he. Yes, there was a bundle, and the paper stuck to the inside. It was candy without a doubt; but where was the muffler? Peter turned the stocking inside out, but the muffler had gone after the rest of the things. The candy alone was faithful.

Peter hastened down stairs. Mr. Morgridge was there getting breakfast ready. Peter eagerly told him of his good fortune. What a chuckle did the old fellow give! it was amazing to Peter. He had never before heard Mr. Morgridge make such a noise. He had never seen his face so broken up into smiles and grins. He could hardly believe it was Mr. Morgridge. Nor was it—it was Morgridge Klaus.

While breakfast was in preparation, Peter climbed up into his watch-tower. Well done! there was a muffler in the chair! precisely like the one which he had seen enter the stocking the night before. How could it have found its way to his seat? As he was looking at it in wonderment, there was another undoubted chuckle from Morgridge Klaus. Peter was astonished beyond measure. Could Mr. Morgridge be Santa Klaus? impossible! yet he began to believe it, for was it any harder of belief than that it was Mr. Morgridge who then spoke in a voice that had in it the cheeriness of Solomon Mit:—

"Come down, little Peter! To-day is Christmas Day. We must hurry through breakfast; for we've got twenty-five turkeys to carry to twenty-five honest poor folk. It will go hard with us, but we'll make shift to buy 'em. God bless you Peter Mit!" and may the Indian in front of the door tomahawk me if David Morgridge did not then and there, in his old, wheezy, snuff-choked voice, sing —

"All glory be to God on high,
And to the Earth be peace,
Good will, henceforth, from Heaven to men,
Begin and never cease!"

The Little Castaways
JULIA'S STORY.

The Little Castaways

IT was a June afternoon, long and gentle; the sun did not scorch as it does in August, and the wind was from the South, just strong enough to stir the trees a little, and to carry the fragrance of the flowers through the air.

It was such an afternoon as old people like to spend listlessly watching the bees and the butterflies, and thinking of old times; nor are they the only people who like June afternoons; their children and their grandchildren in different fashion, make the most of these long hours and never think them too long.

Old Benjy Robin was humming a psalm-tune as he sat in his chair upon the front stoop of his son's house, where he always lived; he had moved away a little from the open passage which led to the back of the house, to avoid the draught of wind that passed gently through. It was a very pleasant wind to younger folk, but Old Benjy was turned of eighty, and not so warm in his blood as to like such cool currents. His cane stood between his knees, over which was spread a large red silk handkerchief, and his hands were folded before him; while his two thumbs slowly turned round each other, sometimes one way, sometimes the other. Before him he could see down the garden walk, with its trim rows of shrubbery, and beyond farther on, the very lovely hills that closed in the lake of Clearwater, the shore of which was but a little way off.

John Robin, his son, who owned the house and farm, owned also part of the lake, and there was a path, leading from the other side of the road in front of the house, down to the shore where the horses were taken to water and where the farmer kept his boats. It was a beautiful view from the stoop, especially when as now the white clouds were floating over the tops of the hills.

It was so quiet and the air was so mild that old Benjy soon began to feel sleepy; he took the red bandanna from his knees and threw it over his head to keep the flies away from his face, and then settled himself to sleep, while his thumbs continued to go slowly round and round as if they were trying in vain to overtake one another. Old Juniper too, the great Newfoundland dog that lay at his feet, gave up trying to catch the flies that plagued him, and stretching himself out as much as he could, drew in his tongue over his red gums, and also fell sound asleep breathing very hard.

The only persons in the house this June afternoon were the old man, Juniper the dog, and Yulee, and Bo, Robin, Benjy's grandchildren. Their father and mother had gone out for the afternoon and would not be back until after tea; the boys were at work at the other end of the farm, and so the children had been left in care of their grandfather and the servant-maids. But Benjy had gone to sleep, and the servants had taken the time to pay a visit to the next farmhouse. The children however did not notice this; they were sitting on the door-step at the back of the house, at the opposite end of the passage to where their grandfather was. They enjoyed the wind that was blowing through so pleasantly, and Yulee was reading aloud from a book to her brother Bo. Yulee was eight years old; her real name was Julia, but no one but the school mistress ever called her so. Bo, short for Robert, was two years younger and wanted to do everything that Yulee did. Wherever Yulee was, there you would be sure to find Bo. He followed her about as faithfully as a chicken does her mother, and Yulee treated him very much as a hen does its only chicken.

The book they were reading was called "*The Castaways*," and Bo was listening to Yulee with the greatest attention. At last, just as the great clock in the hall struck three, Yulee finished; she had skipped some of the parts, especially the hard names and Miss Keenmark's science, but she had read the book through and Bo had heard most of it.

"Bo!" said she, as she shut the book, "I'd like to be a castaway, wouldn't you? It would be so fine to live on the top of a rock and have to go up a rope ladder, and keep goats, and save the lives of Africans, and sleep in an ox-cart!"

"Oh, but the lions!" said Bo, "and the—and the—what are those big things that live in the water, and most swallowed the canoe?—you know."

"I know what you mean," said Yulee. "The hippopotamuses. I said the word all the way going to school yesterday, so as to remember it."

"I shouldn't like them," said Bo.

"Oh, but one of the men would fire right into his mouth, just as Albert did. I'll find the place;" and turning over the leaves of the book, she came to the story, and read:—"But they had not been long seated when a tremendous shock was felt; the light canoe was thrown above the water, and capsized in a moment; and Albert, who was standing at the stern of the raft, watching the boat, saw, to his great horror, the huge head of a hippopotamus raised above the water, preparing to seize the canoe with its red open mouth. Calling for aid, he seized his gun and fired in the face of the ferocious beast, which with terrific roars, dived down and disappeared."

"But who'd you have to shoot the—pippi—what is it?" asked Bo.

"The hippopotamus," said Yulee, who liked to pronounce the word; "why, of course, there must be some men wrecked with me: there's the captain, and the doctor, and carpenter, and the passengers—"

"A'n't girls ever wrecked alone?" asked Bo; Yulee thought a minute; she tried to recollect the different stories she had read about people who were cast away. "No;" she said finally, "there is always the captain, and the doctor, and the carpenter, and some of the passengers at least; and the carpenter finds his chest."

Bo had nothing to say against such a mode of shipwrecking, and Yulee continued: "But I think I'd rather be cast away on an island like Robinson Crusoe or The Little Robinson, where there was water all around, and canoes and pearls, just as it is in 'The Swiss Family.'" "Bo!" she said suddenly, "I do declare! let's be cast away on the island in the lake! We can get into the boat, you know, and be wrecked on the shore, and you can take your bow and arrows, and I'll take my tea-set and my range, and we'll build a little house, and perhaps there are some goats on the island! Wouldn't it be grand!"

Bo opened his brown eyes wide at the idea. "Well let's do it!" said he; it was enough for him that Yulee had proposed it; "I'll go right off and get my bow and arrows."

"And I'll get my tea-set and the range, and I'll take Miss Phely," said Yulee. They jumped up from the flat door-step, and ran into the house, and up stairs to the play-room. There they began collecting what they thought they should need, and Yulee very soon pounced on Miss Phely who was in the corner of the room, sitting very stiffly upon a small willow rocking chair. Miss Phely's face originally was black, but rather streaked with a doubtful colour now, as it had been washed somewhat vigorously at different times; her eyes were blue and very wide open, and her dress, which wanted a pin behind, was of spotted pink calico. Her arms she held rather stiffly away from her clothes, and her fingers were stretched as far apart as they well could be. Yulee was in a hurry, and took her up unceremoniously by the waist, but Miss Phely did not seem at all disturbed, and did not even wink or shut her fingers together.

They hurried down stairs and out by the front door, passing on tip-toe by their grandfather, Old Benjy Robin, who slept soundly in his chair, with his cane between his knees and the bandanna thrown over his head to keep away the flies. Even Juniper, the dog, never woke up, though Yulee was strongly tempted to add him to the party of castaways. They passed through the garden gate, and crossing the road walked through the pasture, down the path that led to the shore of Clearwater. There, tied to a stake, was their father's flat-bottomed boat, with keel-boats near by. Yulee chose the flat-bottomed boat, and they proceeded to put on board their various stores.

First, and head foremost, Miss Phely was deposited upon one of the seats; if her head had been less hard it must have disliked the wooden pillow that it was knocked down upon. After her came the box of cups and saucers, tea-pot, sugar-bowl and creamer; then some of Miss Phely's clothes, in case a change were desirable; a little Shaker basket, never before used, which Yulee said was for berries; the bow and arrows; a pail for the goats' milk; a tin pump with a trough attached to it; little Bo carrying a pop-gun which was too valuable to be suffered out of his hands; and lastly, Yulee holding in one hand "The Castaways," to refer to in case of need, and in the other the most precious thing of all to her—a little complete leaden range with places for every thing, which had been given her for a present on her last birth-day, and in which it had ever since been her secret but firm determination to build a real fire. The range was alto gether too valuable to be laid on the seat like Miss Phely, so Yulee kept it in her hands; and she had not forgotten either—prudent Yulee! to bring some matches wrapped up in a piece of newspaper, and which she kept her eyes on constantly, as they lay in the range, expecting every moment to see them start a-fire; indeed, they kept her very uneasy. However, everything was now aboard.

"Here, Bo," said she, "you sit down there, side of Miss Phely, and don't let her tumble overboard, and I'll go and untie the rope." Bo began to be a little frightened, but he had faith in Yulee, and Yulee had great faith in herself. When she had untied the end of the rope that was in the boat—and very hard work she found it—she said:

"Now we're off, Bo! are you all ready?"

"Yes," said Bo.

"No; you must say, 'aye aye, sir!'" said Yulee.

"But you a'n't *sir*," said Bo.

"Yes I am," said Yulee, "I'm the Captain;" and she took her seat in the middle of the boat, where she said the Captain always sat. "This ship is the *Little Madras*, Bo," said she. "Where's 'The Castaways'? I'll read about it." So she read how all the party, after their first shipwreck in the *Madras*, had embarked again in the ship's long boat, which the Captain called the *Little Madras*.

"Are there any of those big animals here? you know that long name," asked Bo.

"Hippopotamuses?" said Yulee, promptly, delighted at the opportunity of using the word. "Oh, no! there are no hippopotamuses in Clearwater; the hippopotamuses only live in Africa."

"You never saw one, did you?" said Bo, who didn't like to use the word.

"No," said Yulee. "I never saw a hippopotamus, but I've seen an elephant in the menagerie and I guess it's something like it. There's a picture of one in the Castaways," and she showed it to Bo.

While they were talking, the wind and the current had been gently drifting the boat away from the shore; they were quite a distance from the stake now, and really going toward the island, which lay in the lake not very far off. They had never been there for their father said there was nothing to see on it; but Yulee was very certain in her own mind that there was something on the island very wonderful. She had made up a great many stories about it, which she had told over to herself so often that she believed them as much as if some one else had told them to her. She was sure that there were goats there at any rate and possibly a parrot; and she was ready to believe in a cave, and perhaps even a small mountain with a rope ladder up to the top like the one in "the Castaways," though she rather thought she would have seen that if there had been one, from the shore. The island could not be seen from the house, nor from the boat-landing; it was round a curve in the lake.

The boat followed the current which led it slowly toward the island, and Yulee was in ecstacies as they neared the shore. She sat in the bows of the boat looking eagerly toward the island and trying to make out a good place for a cave. But the land looked rather unpromising; it was low, rising but little above the water, and covered with grass, a few low bushes and one clump of trees. The boat did not seem able to get much nearer the island, after it was within a few yards of it, and even appeared to be drifting away. Yulee noticed this and began to be alarmed lest they should not be cast away after all.

"Why don't we get wrecked?" asked Bo at this juncture, leaning over the boat side and looking into the water which was hardly a foot deep here.

"There ought to be a great wind," explained Yulee, "and a storm, and the ship ought to go to pieces, and then we should be thrown on shore, and in the morning we should go out to the wreck and get the carpenter's chest and all sorts of things; at least that's the way it usually happens, but we're in a boat you see, and that makes a difference. I think, Bo," she added, "you'd better take off your shoes and stockings, and get out and pull the boat ashore, or we never shall get there."

So Bo rolled up his trousers, and with some difficulty got over the side of the boat into the water. The boat moved easily, and Bo in great glee pulled it to the island, to a place where there was a little beach, till the bottom of the boat grated on the gravel.

"Here we are!" said Yulee. "Now, Bo, we must get the things ashore before the *Little Madras* goes to pieces." Bo stood on the beach by the boat while Yulee handed to him the various stores and provisions, not forgetting Miss Phely, who was still as wide awake as ever, staring before her without winking and keeping her fingers stiffly apart in the same uncomfortable fashion. Bo took her by the arm and tossed her upon the ground in a very unfeeling manner. Last of all came Yulee, holding fast her precious range and dividing her attention between the dangerous matches and the disembarking from the boat.

"Now, is the *Little Madras* going to pieces?" asked Bo.

"It ought to," said Yulee, "or else it will drift away in the night time. We'll tie it here, though, because you know we may want to sail round our island, and I don't see any log of wood here to make a boat out of as Robinson Crusoe did. Where's the rope, Bo?" she said, as she looked round in vain for it in order to tie the boat to the shore.

"You untied it," said he.

"So I did," said she, "but I must have untied the wrong end. Well, I guess the boat will stay here." Secretly Yulee hoped the boat wouldn't stay; it would be so much more like a real wreck.

"Now, the first thing we must do," said Yulee, "is to explore our island and see if there are any savages on it. You give me the bow and arrows and take your gun, and if you see a savage you mustn't fire at him, but must wait a moment to see if he won't come and kneel down and be your slave."

Bo was frightened at this; he wasn't prepared for savages. "Do you really think, Yulee," said he, "that there are savages here?"

"I don't know," said she, "I've never been here before, but it's best to be prepared. Don't you be afraid, Bobo," she added encouragingly; "you know we can take to the boat if they chase us, and they'll fire darts, but the darts will fall into the water all around us, and won't hit us at all."

"Do you think it's safe, Yulee, to leave the things so on the beach?" asked Bo, as they started off on their tour of discovery.

"Oh, yes," said she, "nobody will touch them, they never do; besides, I've got the range with me." To be sure, she had the range in one hand, but she had left the matches upon the beach as causing too much anxiety. Thus they set off. Yulee with the range and the bow and arrows, and Bo with his pop-gun. It did not take long to explore the island; it was only about an acre in all, and irregular in shape. They came to the clump of trees but did not dare go in, though Yulee was pretty sure that the cave must be in there. They left that, however, for a future tour, and came back without further adventure to their landing place, where they found their stores safe upon the beach, but the boat to Bo's consternation had drifted off from the shore, and was now some distance away, floating down the Lake.

"Oh, Yulee!" said he, "what shall we do I see the boat is gone!"

"That is all right," said she cheerfully. "I wouldn't have been half so much of a wreck if the boat had stayed. A'n't you glad we have got all the things out? The next thing we must do is to build a house."

"I'm hungry," said Bo.

"Then we'll have dinner first," said she. "We'll have strawberries to-day, but to-morrow we'll have fish, or you can shoot a goat."

"But there a'n't any goats," said Bo.

"Yes there are; they're in the cave in the clump of trees yonder." Bo couldn't dispute that, but he demurred as to going in there to shoot them. At present, however, they satisfied themselves with eating strawberries, which were very plentiful upon the island.

When they had eaten their strawberries, and had become quite crimson about the mouth and finger-tips, they returned to the landing-place, where Miss Phely had been keeping watch over the stores. She had been placed in a sitting posture, leaning against a stone, and looking out upon Clearwater as wide awake as when she had been put into the boat, and with her arms and fingers extended as if she were delivering an oration. She paid not the slightest attention to the valuables placed under her guard. Bo began to look about for stones to throw into the water while Yulee thought it a good time to attend to Miss Phely's toilet; so she set busily to work changing her frock; when she had finished this to her satisfaction and was debating whether it would be well to wash her face also, she remembered suddenly, what she had forgotten for the while, that she was a cast away.

"Bo!" she cried, "we ought to be building our house."

"What shall we make it of?" said he. She reflected a moment.

"Sometimes they build them of trees and sometimes of skins; the best way is to have a cave. I wish we had a cave, Bo. I've half a mind to try those trees. Will you go in if I will?"

"Ye-es," said Bo, hesitatingly; "but you must go in first."

"Let's make a fire first in the range and have some tea," said Yulee, who could not quite get up courage enough to go in among the trees.

"Oh, do! that'll be fine!" said Bo, joyfully. It was a very important business, this making a fire in the range. Yulee had long been looking forward to it, and now that she was really about to have the fire she proceeded very cautiously, Bo standing ready to help her and peering anxiously into the process. The range was precisely like a real range, only it was very small, and was made of lead instead of iron. It had a grate in the middle for the fire and a place underneath to hold the ashes; it had ovens at the sides; it had flues and dampers and a chimney piece, and even a place in front to heat irons on; moreover, it was furnished with a full set of pots and pans and kettles. In fact it was complete, and in Yulee's opinion, only needed a fire in the grate, real smoke coming out of the chimney, and a kettle of water boiling over it, to make it the most wonderful and perfect thing that ever had been conceived.

Now she set about preparing the fire. First she laid in the newspaper in which she had brought the matches; then Bo was sent off for leaves and came back with some very green grass and leaves of different sorts. Yulee put these very carefully above the paper, and on top of them she laid some twigs that she had broken up into bits, and now the fire was all ready to be lighted.

"Now, Bo," said she, "we must have the water in the kettle and on the range before we light the fire." So Bo took the pump to the lake side and filled it with water, and then hanging the kettle under the nose of the pump, he jerked the pump handle and made the water come plashing out into the kettle. He could have filled the kettle much easier by simply dipping it in the lake, but it would not have been near so good fun. However, it was full of water, and Yulee carefully set it in its place upon the range. Everything now was ready for the fire. Bo held his breath as he leaned on his hands and knees, eagerly watching Yulee while she proceeded to handle the dangerous matches. She took one in her hand and was just about rubbing it on a stone, when she stopped.

"Bo!" she said, "I think we had better set the table first for tea."

"Why, no!" said he, "mother always sets the table after she has set the kettle a boiling."

"But I shall want to watch the fire," said Yulee. —"Yes, I think we had better set the table first." So the match was laid down to Bo's grief, and Yulee proceeded to unpack the box containing her tea-set. They chose for a table a flat rock sunken in the sand, and just the right size. On this they arranged the cups and saucers, and tea-pot and sugar-bowl and creamer.

"We ought to have some real sugar," said Bo.

"So we ought," said Yulee. "There ought to be some in the ship's stores," she added. "They generally find a box of sugar on the beach, a little damaged by the water. At least I believe they did in Swiss Family Robinson."

"Did they in 'The Castaways?'" asked Bo.

"No," said Yulee, "but you know they weren't exactly wrecked the second time —Dr. Cameron went out to the ship when the rest were on shore, and brought back some things—I think there was sugar; let me see—here it is," and she read:—

"When the watering-boat touched the coast, Dr. Cameron went up and courteously requested to be allowed to return in it, as the ladies had forgotten some little necessaries, and he proposed to bring out their own boat, the *Little Madras*, to enable them to procure these trifles as well as the cooking-apparatus which would be useful if they were detained a few days on shore." Mum, mum, mum. "They succeeded in lowering their own boat, with its oars, and by Marshall's advice, brought from their property the carpenter's chest, disguised under the covering of a travelling trunk, with the powder and shot, ropes and straps, which had been left in the hold of their boat; but every morsel of provision, biscuit, wine and flour had been removed, and could not be found. Dr. Cameron had fortunately locked up his cabin before he left the vessel, and was able to remove his own private property consisting of a bag of coffee, a loaf of sugar, and a chest which contained his valuable medical stores, all of which he now placed in the boat."

Our castaways, however, had to content themselves like some of their betters with sand for sugar, which they put in the sugar bowl, and then filled the creamer with water, though Yulee declared that some time they would find the goats and milk them. The table was now set and Miss Phely was given a place by it, where she sat, still looking out on the water in an abstracted way, and keeping her hands away from her clean frock. She had none of the friskiness commonly belonging to black children; she was anything but a Topsy.

Nothing now remained to be done but to light the fire and make the tea. Again Yulee took a match and Bo stooped down, breathlessly watching the operation. "Ritzch!" went the match and Yulee held it between the bars of the range to light the fire; it didn't seem to burn very well though there was considerable smoke; in fact, the match after burning to the edge of Yulee's fingers went out, and the fire was not yet fairly kindled. Yulee tried another match with about the same success, only a little more smoke.

"Burn a lot at a time," suggested Bo. So she took a bunch of six and got them into a fine blaze. Bo was still peering anxiously while Yulee with her face very red, and her sun-bonnet fallen back, held the bunch of matches between the bars; she tried them first between two and then between another two. All at once something hot fell upon her hand; she dropped the matches in the pan that was to hold the ashes and clapping her other hand upon the spot, began hopping up and down with the pain but determined not to cry.

"Why! what is the matter?" said Bo, in great surprise. Yulee didn't dare trust herself to speak—she was so afraid she might cry, but uncovered her hand to show him, and there they both saw—for she had not looked at it herself yet,— a shining spot as large as a three cent piece, and that looked like silver.

"Why!" exclaimed Yulee.

"Oh!" said Bo.

Yulee forgot her pain for a moment. How did it get there? what was it? she touched it and found that it came off easily. It was irregular at the edges, looking in fact like a spatter of silver.

"What is it?" asked Bo.

"What can it be?" said Yulee. "It looks like silver." She looked toward the range to see if that could explain it. Then she burst into a loud cry.

"Oh, Bo! Oh, Bo!" said she, "the range! the range!" Alas, the matches that had been dropped into the ash-pan, had burnt on and flamed up, melting the lead bars, the first drop from which had burnt poor Yulee's hand. The sticks in the grate had fallen through with the heap of matches, and catching fire, the melting had gone on until now the beautiful range was a sad sight to behold. The kettle just then gave way, and tipping up, spilled the water over, which hissed on the molten lead and caused a great smoke to rise from the burning embers.

Yulee and Bo gazed wofully on the ruin before them. It was too hot at first to touch, and they stood for some time in front of it, looking at the odd shapes that the melting lead had taken. If it had not been for that, they would have been much worse off; but the drops of lead were so curious and looked so much like animals and pieces of silver, that they almost forgot for the time their great loss. But they soon remembered it again and looked sadly at the range.

"Don't you suppose it can be mended?" said Bo.

"I don't know," said Yulee shaking her head, "I don't believe it can. What will mother say!"

"Yulee!" said Bo, suddenly, "I think we ought to pump on it so as to put the fire out." So he ran for his pump which had not been emptied in filling the kettle, and though the trough was somewhat in the way, he managed to spill out the rest of the water on to the hot range, while Yulee brought the cream-jug and emptied its contents also on it. By this time the range was pretty cool and they could handle it; but it was in a sad state, quite melted out.

Yulee tried to solace herself with making tea for Miss Phely; but it was miserable comfort to make tea with cold water that had not even made believe boil as usual on the wonderful range. As for Miss Phely, she was as unconcerned as ever, and seemed equally indifferent whether the water were hot or cold, or even whether the tea were made or not, and sat staring out upon the lake.

But June afternoons, long as they are, have an end at last; and this afternoon was drawing to a close. In the eagerness of making the fire, the little Castaways had not noticed how late it was growing, but now, when they were so disappointed and were sitting with Miss Phely disconsolately by the rock, they saw that the sun had set, and that evening was closing in.

Yes, the night was coming; they had hardly thought of this before and were not at all prepared for it. But it was still warm, for the June afternoon lingers long and far into the evening. Then they fell to eating strawberries again, for make-believe tea where everything is water and sand is not very satisfactory. After the strawberrying they came back to the shore again, and little Bo, now quite disheartened began to make a noise which sounded a little like crying, it was a whimper; but Yulee was brave and kept her courage up, and began telling Bo stories which she had read about people who had been cast away upon islands; but somehow or other she always seemed to remember best the parts where they were attacked by savages and wild beasts, and especially by her favourite hippopotamus. So that Bo only grew more terrified and as it became darker began to fancy he heard ani mals around them, and once actually thought he saw a great hippopotamus with open jaws coming out of Clearwater toward them. Yulee tried to read "The Castaways," but it soon became too dark. Yet she wouldn't give in to fear, but kept her courage stoutly.

"Bo," said she, "it's getting dark and I think it must be time to put Miss Phely to bed."

"I want to go to bed," said Bo. "I want to go to mother!" and little Bo cried now without any doubt. Yulee bravely kept back her tears and tried to comfort Bo, who soon began to take an interest in the unrobing of Miss Phely, who was put to bed on a very uncomfortable rock—the very one in fact at which she had sat for her tea; but it made no difference to her; she went to sleep with her eyes as wide open as ever.

When this was over, Yulee, never at a loss, began to sing for Bo's amusement and her own comfort. She sang all the songs she knew just as they came into her head. "There is a happy land," "Three little kittens." "Pop goes the weasel," "The sunday-school," and some others which I have forgotten. Would you believe it? Bo fell fast asleep with his head in her lap. Then Yulee felt less badly; before she had been troubled about Bo, but now that he was asleep, leaning so upon her, she felt a courage at having one depending upon her whom she must never desert, no, not even if a hippopotamus, as she said, were to come toward them.

But no hippopotamus came; instead of that, she saw a boat with a light twinkling in it, come rowing down the lake toward the island. The house and the boat-landing could not be seen from the island, because as I said, there was a point of land jutting out, and because the lake too makes a bend. Yulee was singing the song about the little robins as the boat came round the point. She was singing the line

"And what will the robins do then, poor things!"

And looked up at that moment, just as her father catching the sound of her voice—called out:

"There she is! bless her little soul, singing about the robins! Yulee!"

"Here I am, father," said the little Castaway. "Bo, wake up! here's father." Bo gave a sort of snuffle and went to sleep again. The boat with a few pulls was now brought up to the island, and John Robin jumping out, while the boys sat in the boat caught up Yulee and Bo in his arms.

"I've a good mind to give you a good whipping on the spot, you little runaways!" said he; but he did no such thing; perhaps he thought he would leave that to their mother. Bo opened his eyes and blinked in the light of the lanterns, but went right to sleep again on his father's shoulder.

"We didn't run away," said Yulee, "we were cast away in the *Little Madras*."

"Where's the boat, Yulee?" asked one of her brothers.

"Oh that was washed away of course," said she.

"Why *of course*?"

"Why, they always are," said she, "and they make new ones out of logs."

"Why didn't you make one out of a log, then?" he asked laughing. But Yulee was too busy collecting her treasures to answer his foolish question. She got them all safely on board at last, Miss Phely being un ceremoniously huddled into the boat without waiting to be dressed. Now Yulee was reminded of her poor unfortunate range; but she said nothing about it, only gathering up its ruins and taking especial care of it.

Yulee was very talkative at first, but her father was grave and silent, and her brothers teased her, so that she soon stopped talking and began wondering in her mind how she ever was to get the range mended, and whether there was a cave in the grove of trees which she was very sorry now she had not explored; she secretly determined to make a second trip to the island for that purpose as soon as possible.

But when they came to the shore and walked up to the house, and when Yulee found her mother half wild with thinking she had been drowned, and her grandfather, old Benjy Robin, crooning in his arm-chair and saying he had been the death of them,—she began to think it was not so fine, and lay down that night penitently in her little bed and promised over and over never to be cast away again. As for Bo, he would do just as Yulee said, but he privately resolved never to follow her to sea at any rate. Even Miss Phely ap peared so much the worse for her knocking about that I think she must have been better satisfied with her corner in the nursery; but as for repenting of her folly or blaming Yulee, I never heard of her doing so. She always looked contented and indifferent.

A Faery Surprise Party.
LILLIE'S STORY.

MY name is Jack Frost, and I have a story to tell. If you don't know who I am, ask my friend North East Wind, Esq., and he will tell you, and whistle a tune which he made up about me. I am Painter to her Beauty Mab, Queen of the Faeries. She gives me plenty of work to do; in the summer-time I go North, like other artists, to take sketches, but when the winter comes then I come back and paint my pictures. I paint chiefly on glass, though sometimes on pottery, the night is the time I like best to work in, for in the day-time the sun tries to put some colour into the paintings, which spoils them; white is the only colour I ever use.

I was going to tell you, however, a story about what I saw the other night. Queen Mab sent a snow-flake to me with a message. I was to paint eight large squares of glass in a certain window of a certain house. I might paint what I chose only it must be done in good season, for the Queen was to visit the painting when it was finished. So I was at the glass and at work early—'twas only a little after sundown; my friend, North East Wind, jolly old fellow! was whistling a tune right merrily as I handled my brush.

There was a light inside the room, and I could see everything that was going on there; I could hear everything too, for there was a crack in one of the panes of glass; these cracks spoil my paintings—I never can make any mark on the glass close to them—but how ever, here was this crack, and I could make out through it everything that was going on. A nurse was putting a little girl named Milly to bed, and they talked incessantly. Milly was to have a party the next day, which was her sixth birth-day; it was to be her first party. All things had been made ready for it; she had had a new dress, white with red spots like wafers all over it, and she was to wear a red sash and bronze kid slippers. Twelve little girls had been invited, but only eleven were sure to come; Susan Peabody was sick, and might not be there.

All this I heard, and I saw Milly tucked up in bed and left to go to sleep. Then I worked with a will, for I had no time to spare. I begged my jolly friend, N. E. Wind, to be off with himself, as he interrupted my work. So he gave one long wheugh! and away he went.

At twelve o'clock my painting was done. It was the best piece I had done in a long while; one square of glass in particular was superb, though I say it that ought not say it. It was a picture of the palace of Queen Mab; towers and spires were there, hung with crystal bells; the castle was set round with trees, some slim, shooting up above the towers, some stunted throwing out their branches in every direction. The whole glittered most brilliantly. There was a network over all, as if a spider had spun silver threads in front of it. I very often put that on afterwards to add to the effect, though my friend North East Wind pooh-poohs at it; but he knows nothing about art.

It was twelve o'clock, as I said, and the moon was shining brightly; as it rose higher, a moon-beam passed through the window, and through the very square of glass that I had taken such pains with. It passed like a carriage-way right by the great door of the Queen's palace, while the other end rested on the bed where Milly was sleeping. I was standing on the window sash, just touching up the work a little, when, all of a sudden, what should I see but her Beauty Queen Mab with eleven attendants; she came out of the great door of the palace I had painted—that was the finest effect of all.

She got into her sleigh which is made of a dove-feather, curling up in front, and which is drawn by twelve lady birds: the lady birds all had on robes of caterpillar fuz to keep them warm. The retinue of eleven Faeries were all riding on milk-white steeds of dandelion-down. The Queen held the reins herself, and cracking the whip which is made of a musquito leg, away they went over the moon-beam. The Queen saw me just as they left the palace, and gave me a nod. She is very gracious! It did not take them long to reach the bed, I can tell you, and they reined up at the other end of the moon-beam, which rested on Milly's breast.

I wondered what they were going to do here, but it was very soon evident. It seems the Queen knew of the party Milly was to have, and meant to get the better of her by giving her a surprise party first. So she had brought the eleven Faeries with her—just the number of little girls Milly was to have the next day.

The Queen got out of her sleigh, and tied the ladybirds to the strings of Milly's night-cap, that they might not run away. Then she walked along very carefully till she came to Milly's chin. She climbed up it and rested there for a minute, to get breath, and then went on, until she was safely perched on Milly's red lip, where she was nearly blown away, Milly breathed so hard.

Here she beckoned to the eleven and they, leaving their horses below, all set out to reach Milly's forehead, where she told them to gather. A hard time they had of it, too! some of them tried to get up by the nose, but the wind coming out of two great caves was too strong for them; others more wisely crept round by the corners of the eyes, and scrambled up the precipice there. But those who fared worst were a few who tried to get through the hair. They got lost in the forest, and wandered about for a long time, halloing and trying to find the top. You may wonder why they didn't fly—I suppose you think Faeries always do—but I know better. When winter comes they always take off their wings, and put them carefully away where the moths can not touch them—chiefly in old nut-shells; then in spring, their mantua-makers and milliners, the caterpillars and spiders, get them out and put them in repair, or else make new ones.

However, they all at last safely reached the fore head. That was a fine large play-ground for them—the forest behind, and the hill and precipices below. Here they formed a ring and took hold of hands.

Round the ring run,
Pass in and out,
Melt into one,
Puff! turn about!

cried Queen Mab, and in a twinkling the ring of Faeries was going round and round, till it looked just like a glittering ring, perfectly still; then all in a moment they had stopped, and each Faery in turn ran across the ring, ducked between two Faeries, was back again, then between two more, and so on, till I got perfectly confused, and couldn't tell one from another, they seemed so mixed up; they kept getting more and more in a maze, and nearer and nearer to each other, until it was just one solid ball of Faeries; spinning round like a top; then suddenly the ball seemed to burst, and the Faeries to scatter in every direction, but really there was a perfect ring again, and whirling round in just the opposite direction. And then the same thing was done over again, till I should have thought they would all have been ready to drop.

But that came to an end after a while, for they heard the Queen scream, and they stopped to see what the matter might be. It was nothing, though the Queen was a good deal frightened at first. Milly, who was probably dreaming about them, smiled very prettily in her sleep, and as the lip moved, the Queen perched on it almost lost her balance, and came as near as possible to falling into the pit that was open before her. If she had fallen in, she would have struck against Milly's teeth, and that might have been the death of her. She got over her fright soon, and moved a little farther back to get out of harm's way. This put an end to the dance.

After some games of hide and seek when they hid in the eyebrows and the edge of the forest, they had a Tableau. The subject was "The Faery's Sacrifice." That is a favourite story with them. I myself have painted it on glass. A Faery—so the story runs—was once in great danger from a Musquito; it would cer tainly have caught her and killed her, though she was winged and flying very swiftly; but just then a horse of dandelion-down came gliding by; she jumped on it and they two together were too swift for the Musquito and she escaped; but they went so fast through the wind that the poor horse lost almost all his down and finally dropped upon the ground from sheer inability to go further. The Faery loved him so for saving her that she pulled out her own wings and fastened them on the horse;—away he went, and she had to creep home as well as she could. But she did right though she suffered for it;

she was never sorry, and the story is told by the Faeries to their children. This was the story that they played in the Tableau. There were two scenes; in the first the Faery is just mounting the horse to escape the Musquito—the Musquito of course they had to make believe was there, in the second the horse lies panting on the ground and she is leaning over it weeping. There should have been a third, as there usually is, where she puts the wings on the horse, but they had no material with them for that scene.

Then came a Charade. The word was a very easy one—I guessed it myself—it was *Duty*. It was divided into two parts; the first was *dew*. Dew is a drink of the Faeries in summer-time. Half a dozen Faeries sat in a circle. The hat of one of them which was made of a bit of rose-leaf, they twisted and turned till it looked a little like the cup of a violet, though the colour wasn't exact. This they put in the middle; but where was the dew? there was none of course, so one of the Faeries had crept down, got on a dandelion-down horse's back and ridden over the moon-beam to the window. In the crack of the sash he got a wee bit of ice that made part of a drop of water when he held it in his hand. It looked like dew, and he managed to get it safely back without spilling much. This had been put in the hat or pretended violet cup. Each of the Faeries, according to custom, took a spoon in hand and slowly stirred the dew in the cup. The spoons they use are made of pieces of the stamens of different flowers; here they had make-believe spoons made out of bits of hair from Milly's eyebrows. They stirred the dew in the cup, and as they stirred they sang the Dew drinking chorus:—

"The shining Dew in the Violet cup
Flows round and round in a silvery flood:—
Against the sides we'll dash the dew up,—
Then drink! and cool our summer-hot blood."

But though they each in turn lifted the cup, they only pretended to drink, for it was icy cold.

That was for *du*; next came *ty*.

This was done thus. They had a marriage-scene. Two little Faeries stood up together, and the one that was to marry them took a hair from each of their heads, and fastening the ends together, made a long string; with this he tied them together in a true-lover knot; for such is the way the Faeries do when they are married.

This was for *ty*; then came the whole word.

A Faery is seen busily occupied with weaving; she is making a veil for a human maiden which shall keep her from seeing sin; the Faery is singing to herself. Presently up comes a little Brownie—a male Faery that is—most daintily dressed and in the gayest mood. He wants the little weaving Faery to come with him; there is to be a most delicious little gathering in a clover-field on purpose to sip clover-honey—white clover-honey! Now of all things the little busy Faery loves clover-honey; it would be so delightful to be there this charming afternoon. She thinks she will go, but then she remembers the task which the Queen has given her to do—to go would be to disobey. The Brownie still begs, but she is firm—no, she will not go.

That was the whole word—*Duty*.

All this was very simple; a good many would have thought it very childish, but it pleased the Faeries and it pleased the Queen, and that was enough.

But the party had lasted a long time now—much longer than it has taken me to tell of it. The moon path was of course altered, but it didn't make much matter. The Queen ordered them all to take to their horses, and giving Milly a kiss on her rosy lips, she clambered down and untying the lady birds from the strings of the night-cap got into her sleigh. She cracked her musquito-leg whip, away went the lady birds and they passed through the window—how, I don't know, but I'm sure I saw them do it. The Queen saw me again as she passed out, and nodded to me. I had just time to nod back and they were out of sight.

That is all, and if it's not true then my name isn't Jack Frost; and if you don't believe me, ask North East Wind, who is my friend, and he will tell you the same thing.

Wheugh!

The Rock Elephant.

HERE is a tradition among the Elephants that some one of the race will one day mount up to the sky and dwell among the stars. Once a young elephant thought that he must be the one, for a great stone becoming detached from a cliff fell upon his head. He instantly exclaimed, "I see stars all around me. I am surely the Elephant foretold!" and for a few moments actually thought he must have "gone up;" but those standing by saw him rambling round with uncertain step and laughed at him. When he got over the effects of the blow on his head, he had to acknowledge that he was still upon the earth, though he always solemnly declared that for a few moments he really had been in the sky among the stars. Of course he had not "gone up," and each still continued to hope that he was the one destined to immortality. The Lion, they said, was among the stars, and the Bear and even the senseless Dipper. But none knew that to live among the stars one must go through a great deal of suffering.

There were two Elephants living a long time since who were remarkably sagacious. They were married and it was their earnest desire that their son, if they ever had any, should be the one who should climb the sky and live among the stars. They often talked over the best way of securing this good, and ate up an immense number of different kinds of trees because they had heard that there was a particular kind of tree which, when eaten, would furnish the necessary knowledge. Whether they ever ate the right tree or not it is difficult to say, but one night as they were considering the matter, the father-Elephant noticed a strange light in the north.

"Look, my dear!" said he, "surely the woods are a-fire in the north!"

"Oh!" said she, "it is only the moon rising."

"Hold your trunk!" said he, sharply. "Are you such a camel as not to know that the moon never rises in the north?" But on second thoughts, he added, "I don't think it can be the woods on fire. See! the light is streaming up the sky. How many colours it has!"

"Perhaps it is the rainbow," timidly suggested the mother-Elephant.

"Rainbow! your Grandelephant!" retorted he, contemptuously. They stood looking at the increasing light for some time longer with their trunks elevated, the mother-Elephant wisely refraining from further comment; when suddenly the father-Elephant, in a state of great excitement, began whisking his trunk about, and turning, ran his ivory tusks against the large sides of the mother. It was his way of express ing joy. "Have a care!" said she, impatiently, clumsily avoiding his thrusts. "Do you want to make a hole in me?"

"I have it! I have it!" said he, joyfully. "That is the way to the stars! all we have to do is to reach the foot of these Northern Lights, and then there must be some ascent by them to the stars." Hereupon the Elephant began to dance about as well as he could, and tore up several small trees by the roots in his exultation. The mother-Elephant, however, had her doubts.

"I don't believe," said she, "that we shall be any more likely to reach these lights than I was to get to the foot of the rainbow, which you know I tried once and had the mortification of being laughed at by the monkeys in consequence. Nevertheless, I will do as you say, my dear; you know best."

That very night, accordingly, the two set out in search of the Northern Lights. They travelled for days and weeks. Every once in a while, when they began to get discouraged, the Aurora would appear and they would press on with new hope. At last they came to a very cold country. Here they made enquiries of a polar bear. Now the Polar Bear is generally courteous. Like all the family he is very affectionate and always gives one a hearty embrace upon meeting; but he is not sincere. It so happened that his family also had a story and about these very Northern Lights. The story was, that if one could find the foot of them one would discover an immense hole or pit where one could sleep forever. This was precisely what the polar bears most wanted, and they were forever going north in search of the hole. This particular Polar Bear that the Elephants met was at that very time on his way thither. So he thought to himself, "This will never do. If these immense animals reach the hole—for I'm sure that is what they are going for, the idea of the stars is only an absurd blind—they will occupy all the room." This he said to himself, and then he turned to the Elephants and said in answer to their question as to the most direct road —"You will have to keep to the east for some distance; then you will come to ice; cross it and you will come to land again, after which you can again enquire as I am unable to direct you further; though if you go a little south, and call on my cousins, the Black Bears, they will be very happy to give you any information. Just mention my name to them and it will be sufficient." He knew very well that the Black Bears knew nothing whatever of the matter. What they wished was to find the Great Tree up which they could climb and in which they could burrow. But all that the Polar Bear wanted was to put the Elephants off the track.

They thanked him for his politeness, and followed his directions. They came to the ice which they crossed; and once more they trode on land, but upon a new continent—upon North America, in fact, as it is now called. "I am not so sure about this matter of going south," said the father-Elephant. "It seems to me that we shall be going away from the Northern Lights. I begin to mistrust the Polar Bear."

"But my dear," said the mother-Elephant, "surely the way has been just as he told us; and I could never doubt one so evidently warm-hearted. Besides, don't you think it would be best to get where it is a little warmer? You know we don't propose going ourselves; the journey is taken solely on account of our son not yet born. We might let him grow a little in a warmer country and then conduct him to the Northern Lights."

The father-Elephant would not agree with her; he preferred to have his own way; but finally he said: "I think we will go a little farther South, on the whole. I am not sure but there is an easier way of getting to the North, by taking just a little southerly and then an easterly course." This was a very foolish reason, but it satisfied him. All he wished was to do as he chose and not because his wife advised it. It satisfied her too. All she wanted was to get where it was a little warmer; but she found it hard not to say—"that is just the plan I proposed." She was wise not to say it however.

They had suffered a great deal by this time. So much travel and so much severe weather, had brought sorrow and discomfort to them. They were really thin for Elephants. The father-Elephant had lost much flesh, and his skin hung about him very loosely. They complained too of the trees; they were so stunted and such poor eating. They were, in truth, very miserable. They even began to care but little for the object of their journey. The object was changed in fact. Before, they were only anxious to reach the Northern Lights—the staircase to the stars. Now, all they desired was to reach a warmer place—one like that where they once lived.

At last the father-Elephant, overcome by all his trouble died; but the mother-Elephant sustained by the hope of her unborn son, still pressed toward the South, and rejoiced as the days grew warmer. Finally, she reached a pleasant place where the hills were all about her, and the sun shone warmly. Here was born the young Elephant, the son of the two Elephants who had travelled so far. The mother now felt herself very weak.

"My son," she began with great difficulty, "there is a tradition"—but just as she got through the word, she died, and the young Elephant in vain listened for the rest of the sentence.

"What's a tradition? I wonder," he said to himself. "It must be something to eat, I am excessively hungry." He looked round and saw a birch tree standing by. "Ah! that must be the tradition my mother meant, when she said, 'There is a tradition.' Yes, her trunk is pointing to it." So he pulled up the birch tree and devoured it, as well as he could. The young Elephant continued to wander among the mountains but with no great purpose in life; for he was totally ignorant of the story that one of his race would one day mount to the sky and dwell among the stars, so that he was without that great object before him. Neither did he know how much suffering his father and mother had gone through, that he might be the fortunate Elephant who should ascend the sky. It was spring when he was born. The days grew warmer and warmer and he enjoyed them exceedingly. But after a while the days became shorter and the sun was not so hot.

"What is the meaning of this?" he one day asked of a Black Bear with whom he was somewhat intimate.

"It means," said the Bear gruffly, "that bye-and- bye the sun will go a great way off, the snow will be on the ground; there will be no whortle berries to eat, and I shall go to sleep."

"Dreadful!" said the Elephant. "Is there no way of avoiding such discomfort?"

"None that I know of or care for," said the Bear. "Roll yourself up and go to sleep as I do, and you'll be comfortable enough." But the Elephant despaired of ever rolling himself up; he was growing larger every day and such a proceeding was of course becoming more and more difficult.

"Let us call a council of the animals," said he, "and see what is to be done about it." Now the Elephant was greatly feared in the place. He was so large and powerful. So no animal dared disobey when the Hare whom the Elephant had sent brought the message to them. They assembled about a deep pool. The Elephant opened the meeting by dipping his trunk into the pool and squirting water over all the animals. He thought it was great fun, and they did not dare run away, for they feared his anger.

"The Elephant is very good-natured," whispered the Otter, who cared nothing for the wetting, to the Fox who was shivering under his ducking, and contriving a way of getting off. "You never see a large fat fellow but he is so good-natured. What a joke that was of his to squirt water all over the crowd!"

"V-v-very," chattered the Fox. "It isn't what you call a dry joke, though, is it?"

"What a cunning fellow you are!" said the Otter. "But, holloa, are you going off on the sly?" Yes, surely the Fox was starting away.

"Tell the Elephant," said he, "that I'm off after a partridge. We shall want something to eat after meeting." But he did not come back again. While they were all shivering with the wet, the Elephant wiping the end of his trunk upon some moss, opened his mouth and spake.

"I notice," quoth he, "that it is not as warm as it was, and my friend the Bear at my right hand (here the bear sitting on his hind legs nodded his head and growled,) tells me that it will grow much colder even. It would be a great calamity to all of us, and I have called you together that we may confer as to the best means of avoiding this severe cold that is to come, which my friend the Bear (another growl) calls by the name of winter. You are at liberty to make any suggestions you please."

The Wolf spoke first. "Who cares for the winter?" snarled he. "For my part I think it is great sport. The snow grows very hard, and one glides over the crust so swiftly. Besides, it is easy then to see the footsteps of my little friends," and the Wolf leered round upon the smaller animals. "The winter is grand sport."

"But I could not walk on the crust," said the Elephant, "I am too heavy. No, it will not do at all just to take the winter as you would any other season. We must either prevent the winter or protect ourselves from it. Let us hear the Hare. I am not above listening to him."

The Hare came out trembling and hardly dared open his mouth. His friend the Squirrel, however, stood near and clapped to reassure him. "Go it, Long Ears!" said he, encouragingly. Then the Hare bashfully spoke. "My own course is to make a hole and get into it." Saying this, he hopped back to his seat alarmed that he should have said so much.

"That is very ridiculous!" said the Elephant. "It would be quite absurd to expect me to make a hole and get into it." Just then there was a rustling noise over head, and a dark cloud seemingly passed over them. "What is that?"

asked the Elephant. No one answered at first, when the Squirrel came forward in a deferential manner and said: "Please your Bigness, that is a flock of geese flying to the South. They go every winter to keep warm."

"Do they?" said the Elephant. "Why shouldn't I too go South to keep warm?" No one objected to this; they all secretly hoped he would go, except indeed the Wolf, who had been counting on the Elephant falling a prey to him. At last the Squirrel spoke again.

"Please your Bigness, I can show you the way to the South if you wish it."

"Pray what do you know about the South?" asked the Wolf, sneeringly, "How would you go to get there?"

"Follow my tail!" retorted the Squirrel.

"I think I will go to the South," said the Elephant, "and the Squirrel may go with me to show the way. We will start immediately; there is no time to be lost. Stay you all about here till I return." And off he walked, preceded by the Squirrel.

"How thankful I am that he has gone!" said the Hare, "but I wish the Squirrel had not gone with him." The Wolf was savage at the idea of the Elephant's going off and depriving him thus of such a fine winter's provision. He showed his teeth fearfully. And when the night was later, he stole swiftly and silently along the path over which the Elephant and Squirrel had gone. "He will go to sleep," said the Wolf, "and then I will spring upon him." He came up with the Elephant after a while, and found him as he expected fast asleep, with the Squirrel perched on one of his tusks. But the Squirrel kept good watch. He saw the gleaming eyes of the Wolf and knew that he came for no good. Quickly he jumped upon the Elephant's trunk, and running down to the end of it tickled it with his tail. This instantly awoke the Elephant. It was no use now for the Wolf to spring upon him. He could only hope to get the mastery of him if he caught him asleep and off his guard. So the Wolf slunk back into the woods again.

In the morning the Elephant and Squirrel again took up their march. For several days they walked toward the South, until they came one morning to a river that was flowing quietly along. It was not a wide river; it was hardly more than a brook, and one could scarcely hear a sound, it flowed so smoothly. It ran through the forest, its edges skirted with rows of flowers, and its banks cushioned with every variety of moss. There was hardly a large stone in it for the water to eddy about. The Squirrel ran up the Elephant's back, and he in two or three steps waded across. It was not above his knee in any place. Once over on the other side, the Squirrel ran down the Elephant's fore-leg to the ground. The Elephant drank some of the cool water and then amused himself with squirting it about in every direction. He aimed it chiefly at some rocks that lay by the side of the river—rocks of all sizes and shapes. This sport grew tire some, however, and the Elephant began to look about for some new fun. The rocks again met his eye.

"What fun it would be," said he to the Squirrel, "if I should pitch these rocks into the river." Saying this he twisted his trunk round an immense boulder and flung it into the bed of the stream.

"Oh!" screamed the Squirrel. "Don't do so! you will hurt the river."

"It deserves to be hurt," said the Elephant. "What business has it to flow along without making any noise. I'll teach it to sing." He threw rock after rock into the river, piling them high up in some places. The Squirrel looked on mournfully, and could bear it at last no longer. He ran to the Elephant and looked up into his face.

"Do you remember the first night we left home," said he, "how I prevented the Wolf from killing you? For my sake, then, do not destroy or hurt the river!" At this the Elephant grew very angry.

"Go to the Wolf with your nonsense!" said he, and lifting his heavy foot, he cruelly stepped upon the little Squirrel and crushed him to death. The Ele phant was now perfectly fiendish. He raised his trunk in the air and blew a terrible trumpet sound. He hurled rock after rock into the stream. He walked down its side and kept casting in the rocks and stones that lay about so plentifully. The river, when the first stone fell in was shocked by it, and eddied around it in a petulant way. As stone after stone came splashing in, choking its current, the river more loudly complained and remonstrated, but to no purpose. Still the rocks came crushing down, and now the river growing more and more angry, rushed foaming madly along. Over the rocks and between it rushed and roared. The moss on the banks and the tall flowers growing out of it, trembled as the stream rose higher and higher. The Elephant snorted and blew his terrible trumpet, walking up and down, and throwing rocks and trees up-torn by the roots, into the rushing flood. At last the rocks were all thrown in. Not one was left on the banks.

Where now was the beautiful, quiet river? It was turned by the remorseless Elephant into an angry, hateful flood. It was the Mad River. Where was the little Squirrel that had saved the Elephant's life and led him hither, and pleaded for the lovely river that it might be spared? Dead! crushed by the unthankful, cruel Elephant, and swept down the stream that dashed so fiercely along!

The Elephant, after he had done this deed of violence, left Mad River and walked into the woods beyond, cooler in spirit since his anger had spent itself. He began now to reflect upon his conduct. "The river had done nothing to me," he thought, "that I should treat it so harshly. And the Squirrel—I killed the Squirrel, who was my best friend. That was an unkind act." But though the Elephant thus began to blame himself, he never thought of turning back, and undoing as much as he might of the mischief he had done. He kept on his journey and tried to dismiss from his mind such unpleasant thoughts. The Elephant is called good-natured because he is so fat; that may be, but really he is both cruel and cowardly.

He was somewhat fatigued by his angry labours and did not go much further, but coming to a grassy place in the depth of the forest, he lay down and slept. Nightfall came soon after and still he slept. In the depth of the night, when all was still and dark, the sky in the north grew brighter as rays of light shot in quivering ecstasy toward the zenith. It was the Northern Lights—the Aurora Borealis. The parents of this Elephant had long sought it but had never reached it; they had hoped that it would be the staircase up which their son, the Elephant, now asleep, would mount the sky to dwell among the stars. Still he slept, though the light grew clearer and the rays became more distinctly marked. It was now twelve o'clock and deep night. What was that descending the slope of the Auroral Light? Who could tell? Who saw it? Yet the Elephant in his sleep saw it. Down the slope he knew It come—down the staircase which was the way to immortality. Now It hovered near him and thus he heard It speak:—

"Thou hast sinned. The river that flowed so peacefully and carried beauty and joy wherever it ran, thou hast despoiled and rudely ravaged. Thou smotest its breast with terrible rocks; thou wouldst not heed its complaining cry; thou turnedst its peace into mad wrangling. But worse, thou slewest with thine own foot the little one that loved thee and saved thy life from the fierce Wolf. For this the river and the Squirrel shall be avenged. Thou didst choke the river with rocks; thou didst crush the Squirrel with thy foot. Thou shalt thyself become a stone and another shall stand on thy head. Arise!"

The Elephant obeyed trembling. He stood upon his feet. For one moment he saw with his mortal eyes It that had spoken; the next he was blinded by a flash; he saw no more, but he knew that in that instant he was turned into a rock where he was standing. His feet were sunk in the ground and his trunk extended before him was also rooted in the earth. All stone. Where his eyes were, only two slight chinks in the rock remained.

But at the same moment the Elephant heard,—so faintly that he could hardly catch the sound—a last word from the voice:—

"Thus, but not forever. A Deliverer shall come and thou shalt mount up to the sky and dwell among the stars."

That was what the Elephant heard. He heard nothing more but he could feel. He could feel himself a stone; that is a dreadful thing to feel. It was a heavy, crushing feeling; a dead weight always bearing him down. He could not lift it; he could not throw it off. It was forever crushing him down, down,—though he never really sank. But it was the same thing to him; he felt that he was sinking.

But he had another evil to bear. A tree with its roots sunk in the ground all about him, stood directly over his head. That was a bitter suffering to him; he could feel it there. He knew that it was stretching its long arms into the air and waving its branches in the wind. He knew that its roots grappled his body and grew tighter fixed in the earth. The tree, indeed, died in time, but another took its place and the torment grew with it. For it kept in his mind the Squirrel he had killed. He could stolidly bear the crushing weight of the rock bringing remorse at the recollection of the happy river that he had made an angry brawling stream,—but the tree—it was a birch, the very kind that he had first devoured after the death of his mother, the tree, that moving with every breath of air, stirred in his mind the recollection of the Squirrel he had killed, who had loved him, saved him from death, and died beside for love of the river— the tree he thought he could not bear.

But still through all his remorse and bitter anguish, the Elephant seemed to hear, though faintly, the last words spoken:

"But not forever. A Deliverer shall come, and thou shalt mount the sky and dwell among the stars."

This was the only slight ray of comfort, though he did not always remember it, but still when the morning sun arose and its beams fell upon the rock, it awakened the remembrance in the Elephant's mind, and he repeated to himself, "A Deliverer shall come." And sometimes in the deep and still night, the Aurora flushing in the north would lighten up a deeper and more cheering hope, for by it he thought would the Deliverer come.

But though the Deliverer has not yet come, still some small comfort does the Elephant have. For the gentle mosses have grown over his stony body; the mosses on the river bank he had terrified and roughly beaten with the jagged rocks. Now did these spread themselves over him, covering him with green verdure and gladdening his soul with the love they gave him. The tree, too, drops yearly its leaves upon his back, and the roots, though they hug him closer, seem to him to do it more lovingly and not with the old terrible gripe.

Yes, all these things make him mindful of the Deliverer. He knows not in what form he will come, but I will tell you. A Squirrel shall finally gnaw away the roots of the tree and it will fall never to rise again. The river, turning its course, shall flow over and about him, and its constant washing shall wear away the rock. The rocky covering gone, in the night, the deep and still night, the Aurora of the north shall stream upon the bed of the river, and where the rock once stood shall rise up the Elephant, and the Squirrel that once led him shall now go before him and lead him up the quivering rays to the sky, where he shall become a constellation never before seen by men, but then discovered and named.

The Old Brown Coat.
ALICE'S STORY.

I- The Gift.

HE royal family of the Kingdom of Percan had an old brown coat which they prized very highly; it was so old that no one could say exactly when it was made, but the story was that the Phœnix made it for the first King of Percan, so it must have been very old. Only the ruler of the kingdom was allowed to put it on, which he did once a year, on New Year's Day. Anybody else who wore it either would die or become king. Such an old coat would have to be mended occasionally, for though the King put it on very carefully on New Year's Day—sixteen men helping him on with it and taking two hours to do it in—and though he only wore it an hour and then put it away safely in a cedar chest for the rest of the year,—yet for all this care the coat, being so old and weak, frequently was torn. Whenever this sad event happened, the sixteen men who were called "Coat-Tails to His Majesty," (because they were appendages to the coat,) carried the coat to the oldest woman in the kingdom, who was obliged to mend it. If she were so old as to be helpless, the Sixteen Coat-Tails put her to death and then went to the woman next to her in age, who was of course the oldest then, until at last they found one who could mend it. Then they all kept guard over her to see that neither she nor any one else put it on, and when the coat was mended, they carried it back to the king's palace and put it away in the cedar chest. Once safely locked up, the Sixteen Coat-Tails sat on the chest by turns all the rest of the year. They were very trusty men indeed; it was a great honour to be one of the Coat-Tails.

Now, at the time when this story commences, the King of Percan was Shahtah the Great. He was called the Great, because he weighed so much and measured so far round the waist; since he had come to the throne, he had been growing greater and more powerful, until his fame spread through all the earth.

It was New Year's Day; and all the people came flocking to the palace to see the King put on the Old Brown Coat. At noon came a long procession led by the Sixteen Coat-Tails, headed by Kaddel the chief of the Sixteen; they carried the coat in a gold box. "See!" cried the people; "that is the box! the Old Brown Coat is inside! hurrah!" and as the procession passed, all the people shouted and tossed up their hats. And Kaddel was so splendidly dressed that he thought some of the crowd must be shouting for him. Then the palace was crowded as Kaddel at the head of the Coat-Tails brought the box before the King, who sat on the throne, and opened it in the presence of the royal family and the people, who however could not get near enough to see very much. The King who, as I said, was very fat, came slowly down the steps of the throne and laid aside his regal apparel, when the Sixteen Coat-Tails lifted the Old Brown Coat very carefully and began putting it upon the King; and very hard work it was. "I must reduce my size," said Shahtah; "next year I will drink a great deal of vinegar. I really am afraid I shall not be able to get the coat on without tearing it." Indeed the coat was already beginning to burst in several places, and Shahtah became quite heated with trying to make himself as small as possible. "If your Majesty would let out your breath," said Kaddel, "I think we might get it on." So Shahtah let out his breath as well as he could, at the same time shrinking in his skin, and the Sixteen Coat-Tails seized the opportunity to give a final push to the coat, so that it was at last fairly on, two hours and five minutes after it was taken out of the box. But Shahtah, the King, could not possibly do without breathing longer; he grew very red, and by the time the coat was fairly on was so exhausted, and so relieved at being through with the exertion, that he drew a long breath and sighed heavily, which expanded his portly frame until the coat burst in twenty rents. "How vexatious!" thought Kaddel, "and my grandmother who is blind, is the oldest woman! If now, the King were only as thin as I am," (for he was very thin,) "there would be no difficulty; or if I were only the king," he half added to himself.

When the coat was taken off, after the people had looked at it for an hour, and Shahtah the Great had been put to bed, for he was very much exhausted,—the Sixteen Coat-Tails immediately set out with the coat to get it mended. "Who is the oldest woman in the kingdom?" asked one of them. Kaddel kept the list and had to answer—"It is my grandmother." So they went to her house. But Kaddel's grandmother was ninety years old and blind, and besides had lost the use of her hands by paralysis. Of course she could not mend the coat, so there was nothing to be done but to put her to death and find the next in age. The law was very strict and could not be avoided. When they went away with the Old Brown Coat, Kaddel felt very bitter toward the fat old Shahtah. "If he had only been lean like me!" he groaned; "or if I were only king," he added to himself. This he said to himself so often that by the time they had found an old woman who could mend the coat, Kaddel had made up his mind to be king. "To be king," said he, "one must needs wear the Old Brown Coat; to be sure one may die; but the chance is even; and at any rate I am determined to kill Shahtah for making my grandmother die. The coat would just fit me."

The first night after the coat was finished and safely locked up in the cedar chest in the palace of the King of Percan, it was Kaddel's turn to sit upon the chest to guard it. In the middle of the night when all was quiet, he opened the chest and very carefully put on the Old Brown Coat; it was a perfect fit. "Now that I have put it on," said he, "I must either be king or die." Then he wont silently up to Shahtah's chamber where the guard let him in without suspicion, for Kaddel was a very trusty man and chief of the Sixteen Coat-Tails; there he killed the fat Shahtah and came out again. "Do not disturb the King," he said to the guard, "he will sleep late." Returning to the chest he took out the coat again and, doing it up in a bundle, went off with it on horseback long before morning, for he said to himself, "I will escape with the coat, then when the family of the King find he has been killed and the Old Brown Coat taken by me, they will be very angry and try to catch me and get the coat again, for no one can rule who does not wear the coat. But the people like me, and after a while I will come back and rule over them." So he rode night and day for a long while, and though the King's family sent messengers after him in every direction, they could not find him.

But Kaddel had forgotten that he who wears the coat may after all not be king but die. He was in the forest on the banks of a beautiful blue river. He was hiding in a cave very far away from any living person, but not far away from the wild beasts. One day he had taken the Old Brown Coat out of the bundle and laid it upon the limb of a tree, that he might look at it and fancy himself a king wearing it; but a tiger stole smoothly behind him and, before he was aware, the beast had killed Kaddel. The Coat lay still upon the bough and was protected by the leaves. But a great wind came and broke off the bough, send ing it into the river that flowed below; the coat clung to the limb and floated with it for many days down the river.

Now the river ran for hundreds of miles through the forest without passing any house, but then it came to a woodman's hut where dwelt, entirely alone, the woodman and his little daughter Isal. One evening after the sun was down, Isal was playing on the river bank when she saw a limb of a tree floating down the river toward her; as it came near, the current of the stream brought it by the bank, and Isal, reaching out into the water, took hold of a twig and drew to her the very bough which had floated for hundred of miles down the river, with the Old Brown Coat snugly hid among the twigs and leaves. "Here is a coat!" said Isal. "I wonder where it could have come from!" She took it off the bough, which drifted away as she let it go, and held up the coat to look at it. "And what a strange looking coat it is!" she said. "It must be very old; it is very carefully mended too. Some poor person must have owned it; but it doesn't belong to anyone I know. I'll see if it fits me." Now Isal had never heard anything about the Old Brown Coat of the Kingdom of Percan, and of course knew nothing about the story that any one who wore it must rule or die. "It certainly fits me very well," said she, "but I don't think it is very warm; it is soft though, and I will sleep on it to night." She carried it into the house and showed it to her father, who turned it round and round but knew no more about it than she. When night came she laid the coat upon her hard bed so as to make it a little softer, for they were very poor, and soon went to sleep upon it.

Do you recollect that I told you at the beginning of this story that the Phœnix made the Old Brown Coat? Yes, the Phœnix made it, but not the one that was living then; for the Phœnix, you know, lives for five hundred years; there is only one Phœnix at a time, and when the old bird has lived his five hundred years, he builds a bonfire of sweet spices and lies down on it; when he is burned to ashes, out of the cinders rises up a new Phœnix with crimson and golden feathers who also lives five hundred years, and so on. It looks something like an eagle, though to be sure it is a great deal more magnificent than the eagle, and is a very wise bird. I do not know how old the present Phœnix is; persons differ about his age. Now it was a Phœnix—surely the great-great-great-grandfather of the one who was living in the reign of Shahtah, King of Percan, that made the Old Brown Coat; and the descendants of that bird, called generally Phœnix the Tailor, took a great interest in the coat and in all who wore it. The Phœnix who was living at the time of this story, was very much concerned about the stealing of the coat. He was a very old bird; he was four hundred and ninety-five years old when Shahtah was killed, and of course knew a great deal.

"Such a thing has not happened in my memory," said he, gravely, "but the times are growing very degenerate. When I was young there was a great deal more respect shown to the Old Brown Coat. That coat was made by the Tailor, my great-great-great grandfather. I can remember when the whole kingdom would have held their breath if there had happened a rent in the coat. But the times are sadly degenerate. I am sure I don't know what the world will come to after I die."

This he said to the Tufters. The Phœnix of course can have no children, so he generally adopts four birds of some other family and brings them up to wait on him. The four adopted children of the Phœnix were Tufters, that is a kind of goose, but differing from the goose in having a very fine scarlet tuft on the head which sets off the white body very finely; besides the Tufter is very wise. You sometimes hear persons say—as silly as a goose, but never as silly as a Tufter. Still the Tufters are geese after all, and are very fond of cackling. So, when the Phœnix had done speaking, the Tufters looked at one another and burst into a fit of cackling. The Phœnix was very much displeased at this. "How often have I told you," said he, "not to cackle in that way. It is very disrespectful in you. Besides this is no cackling matter." So the Tufters tried to look solemn, which made them look very much like geese. "I don't know exactly what it is best to do about this," proceeded the Phœnix, stroking his beak with one of his claws as he always did when he reflected; "but at any rate we must watch the coat." So the Tufters were sent off to keep watch over the coat, all except the youngest, who remained behind to take care of the aged bird. Her name was Rosedrop, because the tuft on her head was shaped and coloured like a rose.

After a while the Tufters came back very much excited. They forgot to make their obeisance to the Phœnix, when they came in, which irritated the venerable bird very much. "Where are your manners?" said he, sharply, as they were about to speak all at once. The Tufters recollected themselves, and standing in a row before the Phœnix, each upon one leg, they stretched out their long necks and bowed all together till their heads touched the ground, when they rubbed their brilliant tufts in the dirt. They always do this to show their humility. This pleased the Phœnix, and he told them they might speak now if they had anything to tell him, but one at a time. Whereupon, they all forgot their manners again, and cackled together in a most confusing manner, telling him that Kaddel had been killed, the coat had been carried down the river and captured by a woodman's little daughter, named Isal.

"I saw it myself," said the oldest, "and I saw Isal take it from the bough, on which it floated, and put it on."

"Yes," said the second, "and she has gone to sleep on it. She is very beautiful."

"But she will have to die or else rule, which is impossible, though; the law is very strict," said the next.

"Oh!" said the youngest, who had stayed with her father, "and must she die, because she put the coat on?" And Rosedrop looked very sad. She would have cried, but Tufters never cry. The Phœnix was evidently very much perplexed. He shook his head very hard while all the Tufters stood huddled around him.

"We must put this right," said he at last; but he did not say how; no doubt he knew, though, he looked so wise.

"Suppose we carry the coat back to the Prince; he will never know that Isal wore it," suggested the third of the Tufters who had spoken before.

"Little Tufters should be seen, not heard," said the Phœnix; "I did not ask your advice." At this the Tufter who had spoken so rashly looked very foolish, and the rest cackled over it. "You're a goose!" said they, all except Rosedrop, who came up and stroked her brother's tuft with her bill. "Isal must be brought here," at last said the Phœnix. "You must all four go and bring her here with the coat."

Away flew the Tufters—they fly very swiftly—and long before morning, though it was hundreds of miles away, they had come to the woodman's hut. The father and Isal were both asleep—Isal upon the Old Brown Coat. "What a sweet face!" whispered Rosedrop. Then each took a corner of the coat by the beak and lifting it up with Isal upon it, they flew out of the house and back again to the Phœnix. Isal was still asleep, but the morning light would soon wake her.

"Shall I give her a worm?" said the Tufter who had spoken so rashly before.

"Nonsense!" said the Phœnix sharply. "Little girls don't eat worms! Be more discreet. But you may go and find some berries." So he went off for them and Rosedrop with him. Isal was awake when they came back, and very much astonished at everything about her.

"How came I here?" said she, "with these strange looking birds about me. That is certainly a very odd looking bird, and very tame;" and she went up to the Phœnix to stroke it.

"Make your manners! make your manners! Stand on one foot! Put your head out! so!" screamed all the Tufters at once, as they stretched out their necks toward her and the Phœnix. But Isal could not tell that they said anything. "How these geese do cackle," said she, as she stroked the Phœnix, who did not dislike it, though he thought her rather forward, and bade Rosedrop bring her some berries. Rosedrop brought them to Isal, who thought she was the prettiest of all, and not at all like a goose.

"What shall we do with her now we have her here?" asked the rash Tufter; but he was sorry he asked, for the Phœnix gave him a terrible peck.

"I know my own affairs," said the old bird angrily, but really he knew very little about this affair and was sadly perplexed and quite at his wit's end. He said nothing of that though, but looked more than usually wise, and finally, when all were on tip-toe, or rather tip-claw, to hear what the wise bird would say, he spoke, and told the oldest to go to the palace of the King and bring back word of what was going on there.

"Ah!" said the second in age, "the Phœnix is a wonderful bird! what deep plans he has!"

Meanwhile Isal stayed by the Phœnix and the three Tufters, who kept very good watch over her. She looked about in vain for her father's house or for the great blue river; she could not understand how she came to be where she was and in such strange company; for, though the birds all told her everything about it a great many times over, she could not understand them, for she had never learned the Phœnician and the Tufter tongues. After roaming about all day and eating berries, shouting for her father and sometimes crying, she lay down upon the Old Brown Coat. The coat she knew; somehow or other she was pretty sure that it must have had something to do with her strange journey. She had heard her father tell about the wonderful cushion that Houssain rode upon; perhaps she had flown here upon the coat; she would lie down upon it and wish herself home again, and "who knows," said she, "but I shall wake up on my cot in the morning?"

After Isal had dropped asleep the Tufter who had been sent to the palace returned quite out of breath; he had such good news to tell; he hurried through his manners before the punctilious Phœnix, and then proceeded to relate how he had called on his friend, the Peacock, who lived in the palace garden. "I had a very good time, indeed," said he; "we had green peas to eat, and the Peacock showed me all his new feathers. I asked him about the theft of the coat and what the prince was going to do; but he did not know much about it; he said that for his part he thought people made a very ridiculous fuss about a seedy old coat. But just then we were joined by the Rabbit. The Peacock rather despised him; he whispered to me—so loud that I am sure the Rabbit must have heard—'Did you ever see such an absurd tail?' But I am sure the Rabbit is very beautiful and much more intelligent. The Peacock has such a disagreeable voice, and he is always trying to sing. I asked the Rabbit if he knew anything about the coat. He said he did; his friend the Mouse had told him the latest news that very morning; and the Mouse was very good authority, for he lived generally in the library and had gone through a great many books; he was very learned; he had overheard the Prince talking with the prime-minister, and he gathered that the Prince had sent out a proclamation, promising to give a very large sum to any one who would bring back the Old Brown Coat, and if it chanced to be a maiden he would marry her and make her queen; though of course that was quite absurd, the Rabbit said; but then the Rabbit jumps at conclusions. The Peacock tried to turn the conversation once or twice; he thought it was insufferably dull and finally went off in a dudgeon, and I saw him as I flew away, looking very grand, strutting along the garden walk. I bade the Rabbit good-by and left my regards for the Mouse though I am afraid it was rather improper—the Mouse is so learned. And here I am."

When the Tufter finished they all talked very eagerly about what was best to be done, while the Phœnix sat apart and deliberated by himself; of course the four children could know nothing about it.

Finally he called them to him and said—"Children, you may get yourselves ready to go with me to the Palace." This was, indeed, great news; the Phœnix had not, visited the palace for a hundred years. This was indeed a great event!

"May I go too?" asked Rosedrop.

"Yes," said the Phœnix, "you shall all go. You are to carry Isal with you on the coat. We shall go slowly. I am too old to travel very fast."

For a week they travelled. Every morning when Isal awoke she was surprised to find herself in a new place; always with the Old Brown Coat and the strange birds; they only travelled in the night time when Isal was asleep; in the day time they rested on account of the Phœnix. At last one morning, an hour before sunrise, they came to the Palace and alighted in the garden just below the Prince's window. They laid Isal on the Old Brown Coat upon the grass, and then the Phœnix bade the Tufters fly away a few miles into the woods and wait his coming. Rosedrop, however, he bade stay a while, when she tapped with her beak upon the window of the Prince's chamber, and then flew away to join her brothers.

The Prince heard the tapping upon the window, and said—"It is the messenger-bird," and rose to see if it had brought him a billet. He opened the window but no bird flew in, and he leaned upon the sill and looked up to the beautiful sky; the morning-star was just disappearing; he watched it till it was gone, and then cast his eyes on the green grass below. What should he see there but a lovely girl lying asleep on the grass, and a very magnificent bird standing beside her. He hastened down and stooped over the beautiful maiden. "How lovely!" said he; "she is more beautiful than the daughters of Calla. She is the morning-star which I just saw disappear in the heavens." He bent his face to hers and kissed her. With the kiss Isal awoke, and when she saw lean ing over her so grand a looking person, she was more wonderstruck than ever before. "Surely he kissed me!" she murmured. Here the Phœnix broke in with a remark.

"O Prince," said he, "I am the Phœnix. For nearly five hundred years I have lived and guarded the Old Brown Coat. It was stolen, and I have brought it back to you with the maiden you are to marry. But you have taken no sort of notice of the coat. My great-great-great grandfather made that coat. It is more valuable than a hundred lovely girls."

When the Prince heard the Phœnix speak, he turned and saw the grand bird which he had overlooked. But he could not understand a word he said, though the Phœnix spoke very loud and as he thought very distinctly. "This is a very strange bird, indeed!" said the Prince. "Did the bird fly with you from the heavens, Morning-Star!"

Isal said, half to herself, "It is very strange. I cannot understand it at all. How did I come here! It is like a dream. And where are the other birds with tufts on their heads?" She got up as she said this; the Prince lifting her by the hand. Then the Prince saw the Old Brown Coat. "Ah! you have brought me my precious coat again!" said he, and he took it up joyfully. At this the Phœnix grew very much excited.

"He will tear it!" said he. "Where are the Sixteen Coat-Tails? This is alarming!"

But the Prince, without heeding him, took Isal by the hand and led her into the Palace, carrying, too, the Old Brown Coat. Then he made Isal tell him all that she knew about it. The royal household gathered about, mad with joy that the Old Brown Coat had been found again. The Sixteen Coat-Tails came in very solemnly and took possession of it. Each of the Sixteen in turn looked over it carefully, but could not find the least rent or tear. "How wonderful!" said they, "but we are very glad to get it again; we are so distinguished now." The bells of the city were rung and crowds of people came to rejoice over the recovery of the coat. Meanwhile the Phœnix walked about the garden.

"This is as it should be," said he, "as far as the Old Brown Coat is concerned, but I don't receive the honour due to me. I am the Phœnix; the only one of course in the world. I am five hundred years old, nearly. When I was here a hundred years ago I was made very much of. But the world is growing very degenerate." The gardener of the palace came by just then.

"What have we here?" said he. "Can it be that this is the Phœnix? I have heard my father describe the one that was here a century ago, and it certainly was very much like this fine bird." He went into the Palace and desired an audience with the Prince. "Does your majesty know," said he, "that the Phœnix is here?"

At this all the people set up a shout. "The Phœnix! It is the royal bird of Percan! Long live the Phœnix!"

The Prince and people passed into the garden and stood looking at the Phœnix. "Now I am respected;" said he. "This is as it should be." It was a great day for the Phœnix and a great day for the people. The Poet recited a long ode in his honour. The musicians played a great deal of music; the wise men, moreover, all got together and held a discussion for several hours about his age; but the people did not care much for this. The Phœnix was given a place above the throne. And not only that, but upon that very day the Prince of Percan, son of Shahtah the Great, the former king, was throned king and took for his queen the beautiful Isal, daughter of a woodman. He wore the Old Brown Coat, and it fitted him very well; it took the Sixteen Coat-Tails only an hour, with all their care, to get it upon him. When it was nightfall, the Phœnix came majestically down from his high perch, and hovering for a few minutes about the King and Queen, gave them a great deal of good advice which they could not understand, and then sailed grandly away, joined the Tufters in the woods, and flew back to his eyrie, far off. In the Palace lived the Prince and his beautiful Queen, the good Isal.

II- The Sacrifice.

HE Prince and Isal had now been married nearly five years, so that Isal was then eighteen years old and even more beautiful than when the prince found her in the garden. The royal family was at first displeased that the Prince should marry a peasant maiden, but Isal was so good that one could not help loving her, and soon every one said that there never had been such a Queen in Percan. As for the Prince, he loved her more than the whole of his kingdom; he always called her his Morning-Star. And Isal loved the Prince and was very happy in the palace where she had everything she could desire; but often in the five years did she remember the woodman's hut on the bank of the great blue river where she had spent her childhood; often she thought of her father living there alone, reft of his little daughter, the one comfort of his life. Then would the Prince come with his kind love, and quite drive away such sad thoughts. As the years went by she thought less of her former life; indeed it was so different from the present that she persuaded herself that she had died in her cot the night after finding the Old Brown Coat, that now she was in the Paradise she had heard her father tell about, and that the birds—the Phœnix and the Tufters—were the winged spirits that brought her there.

The Phœnix was now very nearly five hundred years old; in a few weeks he would have to build his nest and die. The Tufters too were five years older; but five years makes a great deal more difference with them than it does with the Phœnix. It makes them much wiser; even the one that had been rash was quite prudent now. They waited still on the old bird and brought him all the information they could find about the affairs of the world.

"I wonder how the Old Brown Coat does," said the Tufter who had once been rash, as they all stood round the Phœnix one night. "That was a very grand event we brought about—the marriage of the Prince with Isal. If it had not been for us, Isal might still have been only a woodman's daughter and not a Queen at all!" Here the Phœnix spoke, but with a very muffled voice; his age prevented him from talking very loud or much at a time; he was apt to repeat himself, too, sometimes, and to ramble in his remarks. But the Tufters always listened very respectfully to whatever he had to say: he was so old and so wise; everything he said would bear reflection.

"You are a goose. My great-great-great grandfather made the Old Brown Coat. He was called Phœnix the Tailor. The world is growing very degenerate. I am five hundred years old very nearly. I don't know what will become of it when I die. The Prince is very well, but he did not know me when he saw me in the garden. I was respected, though. The gardener knew me, and the people shouted. My great—"

The Phœnix was going on with some of his reminiscences, or perhaps beginning again, when just at this point there was a rustling in the bushes, and in burst the oldest of the Tufters who had been away hunting for news. All the rest bustled about him as he smoothed his feathers to make his manners to the Phœnix.

"I have some very important news!" began he, with great dignity. "Isal's father, the woodman is dying."

"Is he, indeed!" exclaimed the rest in chorus, except the Phœnix, who stood with one eye shut, painfully distracted between the desire to administer a rebuke and to hear further.

"That may be," said he, finally, "but you should not have interrupted me while I was speaking. Besides you have not told us yet the particulars."

"I was flying up the river," proceeded the eldest Tufter, respectfully, "when I happened to recollect little Isal, and how we brought her away from her house. I was passing the very spot, so I just flew in for a moment, and there I saw the woodman, her father, lying upon his bed very sick. There was no one with him."

"How sad!" said Rosedrop, mournfully.

"The cot from which we took Isal," added the Tufter, "was there still, just as we left it, in precisely the same spot."

"How remarkable!" said the rash Tufter, who had become prudent.

While all this cackling was going on, the Phœnix maintained a stiff silence. At last he stroked his beak with a claw. "Hush!" said the second Tufter, "we shall hear something now." And surely the Phœnix did speak.

"Children, Isal must know of this. We took her away on the Old Brown Coat. My great-great-great grandfather made the coat. He was called Phœnix the Tailor." It was very hard for the Phœnix to avoid speaking of this whenever the Old Brown Coat was mentioned, and he continued for some time to wander upon the subject, till they all thought he was through, and the Tufter, who had once been rash asked: "And who shall tell Isal?" The Phœnix was not really through, though. He was just in the midst of the sentence, "The world is growing very degenerate—" only the last word stuck in his throat—and he was exceedingly vexed that he should be interrupted by an upstart Tufter. "You —" are a goose, he tried to say, but the difficulty in his throat occurred again, and prevented any word beyond the first, and the Tufter taking it for a command to carry the news—he was too quick sometimes,—set off for the palace as fast as his wings could carry him.

"How provoking!" said the oldest; "he will spoil it all with his rashness!" The Phœnix now recovered himself, and having finished his two broken sentences together, "degenerate—are a goose," for he never left anything undone, told Rosedrop to fly faster and carry the news before the other. Rosedrop sped swiftly, and overtaking her brother, went with him in company and soon persuaded him, for he was a good-natured fellow, to let her undertake the message. So when they reached the palace garden, while her brother remained without, Rosedrop flew in at the open window where she had tapped nearly five years ago, and hovering over Isal as she lay asleep, told her the sad message, and flying out rejoined her bother.

"Did she hear you?" asked he.

"Oh, yes," said Rosedrop. "I told her all about it, and she looked very sad indeed. How sorry I am for her. I am sure I shall feel dreadfully when the Phœnix dies."

Now Isal really did hear all that Rosedrop told her; for as the Tufter flew through the open window, a suggestion entered the open window of her mind as she lay asleep, and this is what it showed her:—A lonely woodman's hut in the forest upon the bank of a great blue river; in the hut a solitary man, pale and thin, worn out with sickness and sorrow stretched upon a bed; not a living thing about the house; the axe lying rusty from disuse by the trunk of a fallen tree; one little bed deserted in the other corner of the room, toward which the sick man is turned with longing look, while his lips move but refuse to speak the name his heart dwells upon. And just as the Tufter flew out, having told her message, so did the picture vanish from Isal's mind, and in its place followed others in quick succession, all of them centering about one person—a maiden, who is now playing by the same hut, now surrounded mysteriously by strange birds, now waking to find herself kissed by a noble-looking man, who marries her and makes her Queen of the land. With this she awoke, and saw the Prince leaning over her.

"What were you dreaming about, Morning-Star, that made you look so sad just before I kissed you?" said the Prince. Then Isal told him her dream.

"My father is sick unto death," she said sorrowfully, when she had finished, "and longs to see his daughter." But the Prince comforted her, and told her that he would send messengers who should travel over the whole country to find her father and bring her word of him. So the messengers were sent out in search of the woodman. But the Prince did not know nor Isal, that he lived so far away and so hidden that it would not be possible to reach him before he died.

Meanwhile the Phœnix and the Tufters kept watch over the whole matter. The eldest Tufter returned one night from a visit to the palace where he had seen his friend, the Rabbit. "The Peacock," said he, "would have nothing to do with me since I took to calling on the Rabbit; but I am not sorry, for he is very tiresome and is for ever talking about his tail. The Rabbit is much more sensible, though he has some strange tastes. Do you know, he is very fond of chewing parsley? Is it not queer? I asked the Rabbit what the news was. He said he would ask the Mouse and proposed to me to go and call on him. I was afraid to at first; the Mouse is so learned; but then the Rabbit is on very good terms with him and promised to introduce me. So I got the Squirrel to brush me down—he always carries a whisk brush with him and is very obliging—and went with the Rabbit to call on the Mouse. The Rabbit did not seem at all disconcerted. He was chewing parsley all the way; but I was trying to think what it was proper to say upon entering. "

"The Mouse lives in a very small house; he had to come out to the door to us; it was quite impossible for us to enter. He looked very venerable indeed, and very learned. His hair was brushed back over his forehead, and his whiskers were grown very long. I noticed the Rabbit wore his so; he told me afterwards that it was the fashion among learned men, and though he did not presume to call himself a learned man, yet he thought it best to be in the fashion. I hardly knew what to say to the Mouse; I had been trying all the way to think of some book I might mention, but the Rabbit opened the way very easily. He told the Mouse where I was from and mentioned my connection with you, sir," (turning to the Phœnix; the Phœnix bowed—"Yes, I am well known," he said.) "Ah, indeed," said the Mouse. "The Phœnix? yes. I came across an account of the Phœnicians in a book the other day; the book was elegantly bound; the Phœnicians are a very enterprising race."

"The Phœnicians! indeed!" broke in the angry Phœnix. "There is but one Phœnix. I am the only Phœnix, I am nearly five hundred years old. My great-great-great-grandfather made the Old Brown Coat." And he went on with his reminiscences till he was quite exhausted. After that the Tufter hardly dared mention the Mouse, and, indeed, began to suspect that he was not so very learned after all; but he proceeded to state how he had gathered that the Prince had sent messengers to find the woodman, Isal's father.

"It is in vain," said the Phœnix, who had recovered himself, and was really growing very wise, as the days of his life neared their end. "It is in vain, children, you must go again to the Palace—all of you. I would go myself, but I am getting too old, and besides, I must begin to gather my spices and make my dying nest. This you must tell Isal. Her father longs to see her once before he dies. Yet if she chooses to go to him she must die after him, for she has worn the Old Brown Coat. If she remains with the Prince she shall be happy for many years, and be beloved by her husband and king. If she decide to go, then do you four bear her away to her father."

Away flew the Tufters to the Palace. Again did Rosedrop fly through the window, and hovering over the bed, unknown to the Prince give her message to the sleeping Isal. Again, and at the same time, did a suggestion fly through the open window of the Queen's mind, showing her in succession two pictures: —In one she saw a maiden sitting by the bedside of a dying man in a lonely woodman's hut by the banks of a great blue river; the woodman's eyes are bent on her and all his pain and sorrow are gone; gently he closes his life in the sleep of death; and the maiden alone, with only the dead man upon the bed, sickens also, and lying upon the other cot, slowly, painfully closes her life with no one to hold her hand. Then Isal saw another picture—a Queen in the Palace honored by the people, having everything that she could desire, dearly loved and cherished by the King her husband, and living thus for many years, and when dying at last, wept over by all and kissed at the very moment of death by the good Prince. Then Isal woke up just as before by the kiss of the Prince, who was leaning over her. "You are sad again, my Morn ing-Star," said he. "Be comforted; your father will be found." But Isal did not tell him her dream this time.

"What is she going to do?" asked the rather forward Tufter of Rosedrop, as she came forth through the window again.

"She is perplexed," said Rosedrop. "We will come for her answer to-morrow night." All that day did Isal think over the two pictures she had seen, until at last the second one quite faded from view; only the first remained. "I will go," said she to herself, "even if I must die." The next night when the Tufters came for the answer, they found the window closed. Rosedrop tapped upon it with her beak. Isal within heard it. "It is the summons for me to go," said she. She leaned over the prince; he was asleep; she longed to give him a last kiss. "I will kiss him very gently," said she, but first she opened the window. There were the strange birds again; the beautiful one upon the sill; the rest hovering close by; she went back and lightly kissed the Prince. "Quick!" she said to herself as he stirred. "He is awaking!" She hastened to the window; she stood upon the sill; the birds floated in front of her, and letting herself sink upon their soft downy backs, and throwing her arms round Rosedrop's neck, off they flew, swifter than the rushing wind.

The Prince awakened by the kiss and the rustling opened his eyes only to see his Queen rising like a white cloud to the sky.

"Ah! she is gone! my Morning-Star has returned again to the sky!" he wailed, and stretching his supplicating hands he cried, "Come back to me! My Love! My Morning-Star!" And Isal heard him as she was swiftly borne, and her hot tears fell on Rosedrop's neck.

Just when the morning-star disappeared from the sky before the dawn, the Tufters laid Isal upon her cot in the woodman's hut, and fluttering around her for a moment, they flew away to the Phœnix, leaving Rosedrop only to keep watch. In the hut upon his pallet lay stretched the lonely woodman, who was dying. Day and night did Isal sit by his side and hold his hand while he gazed in her face, too weak to speak. Slowly the pain and the sorrow left his face, and instead came a smile of holy joy which never left him. For seven days and seven nights did Isal sit beside him. Then he died, and she, just able to reach her old cot, lay down upon it, weak and suffering. For seven days and seven nights did she lie there, racked with pain. This was a sad exchange for her happy life in the Palace; but she never repented; she could not when she saw the dead face with its heavenly smile still upon it.

"Isal is fast dying," said little Rosedrop sadly, as she flew back from the hut to the Phœnix and her brothers. "Oh! she suffers dreadfully."

"That must be so," said the Phœnix wisely. "It could not be otherwise." The Phœnix now was so old that in an hour he would die. He had gathered his spice and built his nest; already had he taken his seat upon it, and was awaiting the last moment of the five hundredth year, while the Tufters stood around sorrowfully, each upon one leg, manifesting their respect to the old bird by making their manners constantly; it pleased the Phœnix so much. And the grand bird as he neared his end grew more and more wise and prophetic.

"Rosedrop!" said he to his favorite Tufter. "Go quickly to Isal's cot. She will die; but when she dies, watch for her spirit and bear it hither ere I die." Swiftly sped Rosedrop to the hut by the river. There she watched by Isal's bedside; saw her go through terrible suffering, but at last the struggle was over, and Rosedrop saw through her tears, which she shed for the first and only time, Isal's spirit floating upward. She clasped it to her bosom and darted to the Phœnix.

"It is the hour!" said the Bird, before Rosedrop had returned. "My life is closed. I have lived five hundred years." He plucked a golden feather from his breast, and lighted the nest of spices on which he reclined. The smoke rose slowly, enveloping him in it, while the Tufters, overcome with grief, forgot their manners, and stood on both legs peering into the smoke. At that moment Rosedrop, with the spirit of Isal, darted into the circle. The Phœnix saw her.

"Lay the spirit in the nest," said he, and Rosedrop heedless of the fire which burned her beautiful body, laid Isal's spirit in the nest by the Phœnix.

"It is enough!" said the Phœnix. "I am perishing, but another Phœnix shall arise and the spirit of Isal shall live in it. Isal is the Phœnix that is to be. I die but she shall live."

As he said it, there was a smouldering in the nest; a heap of embers enveloped in smoke lay before the Tufters; in a moment the smoke parted and out of the embers soared with crimson and golden plumage the new Phœnix!

But the new Phœnix remembered still the life that belonged to him when he was a maiden. The Phœnix, moreover, is a most wonderful bird. It can change itself into many shapes. Every New Year's Day did this Phœnix visit the Palace and present itself at the Festivity of the Old Brown Coat, and every New Year's night, after the Sixteen Coat Tails had robed and unrobed the lonely Prince with the greatest care, did the Phœnix visit the Prince alone, and for one night he returned to the old shape of the beautiful Isal. And when the Prince died he was changed into a palm-tree, and the Phœnix dwelt in the branches.

New Year's Day in the Garden.

Morning.

IT may not generally be known, yet so it is, that New Year's Day in the Garden varies each year, but is established by one sure sign—the blooming of the Lilac. When this takes place it is the custom of the inhabitants of the Garden to celebrate their New Year's Day. In the year when this happened which I am about to tell, the Lilac was later than usual, and there was great impatience felt at its slowness. Some of the younger ones, in fact, had serious doubts whether it would come to flower at all, and that they agreed would be a calamity, but the older ones bade them wait, for the time certainly would come. The old Buttonwood tree that stood in the corner of the Garden, and who was said to be the oldest inhabitant, grew very tiresome, for he counted up on his branches the number of years that he had seen the Lilac blow, and declared twenty times a day, as if he had not said it at all, that he had never known the bush to be so tardy. But on the night before the twentieth of May there was a plenteous shower; the next morning the sun rose splendidly upon the fresh earth, and the Lilac sent its strong perfume all over the Garden. It was unanimously agreed that New Year's Day had come at last, and that there should be an unusual celebration of it.

Now listen and you shall hear how the day was celebrated. It was divided into two parts; the first part was the morning, and was occupied after the manner of the inhabitants of the Garden in giving and receiving calls.

Owing to the slowness of the Lilac, many of the fair ones were not so elegantly dressed as they had hoped to be and were quite mortified; but the shower in the night had freshened them and taken away much of their faded appearance, so that none but the most fastidious of their visitors could detect any failing. The Garden walks were quite lively with such of the callers as were obliged to walk, while those that kept their wings, and so could fly, were moving in the air in every direction. The Bee, in his shining yellow coat, was rushing about making a great to do and acting as if no one were of so much importance. He made his first call upon the Rose, who was dressed in a charming robe of a blush-colour, and who received a great deal of attention.

"The compliments of the Lilac to you, my dear Miss," said he, bustling in. "I am a business character; have fifty calls to make and so have commenced early, as you see. What a disgraceful thing it was for the Lilac to be so unpunctual. Really I lost all patience with it. Prompt is my word. 'Improve each shining hour,' you know, my dear Miss, as the poet somewhere says, so I bid you good-morning," and the corpulent fellow in his yellow coat buzzed graciously to the Rose and hurried off to pay his respects to the next on his list.

As he went out, in came the Butterfly and the Moth, who made their calls together. The Moth was clad in grey, and the Butterfly liked that, because it set off his own brilliant colours so well.

"*Bon jour, mademoiselle!*" said the Butterfly, who always spoke in a foreign tongue when there was no need for it, and then he continued in his own, for he was not very perfect in the foreign tongue after all. "How charming you look this morning! What shall we do to the Lilac for denying us so long the sight of your beauty? I say, Moth, we shall have to attend to that fellow." The Moth, who remained in a corner merely bowed and smiled; he was not so brilliant as his companion, and besides was always in a state of anxiety about his coat, which was liable to be rubbed.

"Oh, Mr. Butterfly," said the Rose, "the Lilac is not to blame, and the day is all the more charming for being a little later."

"It is not the day that is so charming," said the Butterfly with a smirk. "But we have a few calls yet to make—seventy-five or a hundred, say. Come, Moth. *Au revoir, Mademoiselle,*" and they fluttered off. "Did you see her blush, Moth, when I said that about the day not being so charming?" said the Butterfly. "That's what they like. Halloa! there goes that simpleton of a Humming-Bird. He thinks he's got the gayest coat in the Garden. What a conceited fellow!"

He said this loud enough for the Humming-Bird to hear, but that graceful creature took no notice of it. He also was out, but he made only one call, and that was to the Honeysuckle, for they were betrothed. Of course it never would do to say what they whispered to each other.

The Spring Crocus also kept open house, though she was so old that the others said it was all affectation! But she dressed herself in a yellow dress, which, however, did not make her look any younger. She had one caller. It was the Grasshopper, who was clad in his major's uniform. He came along the Gar den walk that led to the Crocus in a very formal fashion, taking step with great precision, for he went exactly the same distance at each spring, and halted the same length of time between the jumps. The last spring—for he had calculated it exactly—landed him by the Crocus. The Crocus, who had watched him coming, was highly flattered though rather flustered. It was the first call she had received that day, and she had even feared she might not receive any.

"Your most obedient, madam," said the Grasshopper, lifting his elbow.

"Yes, a very warm day," said the Crocus, not quite at her ease.

"The Lilac is later than usual," continued the Grasshopper.

"Oh, yes, the Lilac, yes," said the Dowager Crocus, "quite so,—the Lilac, oh, yes! it is certainly very wrong. You are looking uncommonly well, Major," and she began to recover her composure and to look less heated.

"Thank you, madam," said the Grasshopper, raising his elbow again, "and I must say that I have never seen you looking better, and, if I may be allowed to say it, younger."

"Oh, la!" exclaimed the Dowager, quite confusedly and getting into a heat again.

"Do you find your company agreeable this morning?" asked the Grasshopper, to change the subject. He referred to the calls she was supposed to have received, but the Crocus thought he referred to himself, for she was still a little off her balance. She was just thinking how she could say something witty, when the Grasshopper added—

"You have had a number of calls, I presume?"

"Oh, yes! a great many. I am quite tired out," said she, though she ought not to have said so, for it was not true, and besides, it might be construed into a piece of rudeness. But the Grasshopper knew she had had none though he did not say so. He had nothing more to say, however, and he bade her good morning, and jumped by measurement down the Garden walk.

This was the first year that the Pansy had received calls and she was quite excited. She was very pret tily pressed in a purple bodice with white skirt and yellow slippers. "Some one is coming!" she exclaimed to her mother, who was not far off. "I can hear a step on the Garden walk." "Be composed," said her mother, "Is your bodice smooth?" She felt of it and it was. The Red Ant and the Black Ant had come in company. The Red Ant is a clerk and the Black Ant is his uncle and an undertaker. They both entered at once and were graciously received. The Red Ant is so methodical and so used to system, that he had arranged beforehand with his uncle precisely what they should say and in what order. So the Black Ant advanced and said quite soberly:

"This is a very lovely day," and the Red Ant immediately added—

"The Lilac is much later than usual this year."

"Isn't it!" said the Pansy very eagerly. "I declare I thought it never would come out. Mother told me over and over again not to be so impatient but I did get so vexed!"

"It makes very little difference with us," said the Red Ant whose turn it now was; "every thing is arranged in the Hill so perfectly that nothing can put us out. We each of us carry fifty grains of sand a day."

"Oh, how severe it must be for you!" said the Pansy. "I don't believe I ever could live so systematically. It is so nice just to enjoy the air and the sun without thinking much about it. Don't you ever get a holiday?"

"It is my turn, you know," whispered the Undertaker to his nephew, and the Red Ant was so systematic that he did not answer the question, for he had forgotten to allow for it in his calculation. So the Black Ant next said—

"It makes no difference to me either. In my profession, though we cannot of course be quite so systematic as my nephew here, yet we make it a point to be at our post, rain or shine. Nephew, it must be time for us to be going."

"Yes," said the Red Ant, "it is exactly time. We allow five minutes for each call and ten minutes between each place. Good-morning!" and they marched off and said exactly the same thing at the next place.

The Pansy thought it was not quite so interesting as she expected, though it was pretty good fun, but soon she had a call from the Dragon-Fly, and that was worth while. So the morning went by, and was fully occupied with giving and receiving calls. Every one professed to have had a very good time, though the Earthworm to be sure had not succeeded in making a single call, he moved so slowly. The Bee was through long before noon, and boasted of it. "Prompt is my word," said he, "I made fifty calls, at an average of fifteen calls an hour."

That was the way they celebrated New Year's morning.

Evening.

IN the evening it was different but no less gay. Great preparations were going on under the Lilac-Bush. Beetles had been at work all day clearing the grass and putting things in order. At nightfall the Turtles and the Frogs sounded the chimes, and a merry noise they made of it. The Catbird rang only one bell. Something evidently was to occur. A little later the glow-worms began to collect, and the place was illuminated. The Lilac-Bush was hung with quantities of them, and others darted about in the air as if they were on the most important business. The Cherry Blossoms in the tree nearby were very curious to know what it all could mean. One of them agreed to go and find out. He sailed down gently and into a cluster of Lilacs.

"This is the grand celebration," said they in answer to his question. "For one night in the year the Little People are coming out for sport before midnight. The Queen will be here, and we are to drop leaves upon her." But the Cherry Blossom was unable to carry the news back, for the winds were not favourable. It was as the Lilacs had said. This was the Queen Faery's reception night, being the first night of the year, and it was under the Lilac that she was to receive her subjects and their gifts.

At last the procession approached, attended above and at all sides by myriads of glow-worms. Foremost came a body of Daddy-Long-Legs, who walked marvellously fast, and cleared the way for the proces sion. Then a band of crickets followed all in uniform, and every one kept step to their music, though that was a difficult matter. Behind the band was the Queen Faery driving as usual her twelve Lady-Birds, which drew her acorn carriage; she was attended by a body-guard of Dor-Bugs, all in coats of mail. Then came troops of Faeries, some mounted, some on foot. They bore banners spun by the most skillful spiders and silk-worms, each company having its own device. For there were Faeries from the woods, from the streams, from the flags in the marshes, from the tops of the firs, from the sea, from the inside of caves, house-faeries, church-faeries, and gypsy faeries, that lived wherever they pleased and were always trespassing.

The fire-flies made it very light and there was no difficulty in finding the Bush. There they halted, and when the Queen alighted she found a delicious cushion for her to step upon; it was the messenger Cherry Blossom which had dropped upon the ground for that purpose. The Queen's throne was a dandelion flower and a regal throne it was. The Spider spun a wind ing staircase to the top, and stretched a canopy over it that glittered with diamonds of dew. While she was taking her seat the cricket band played the Throning of the Queen—one of their finest pieces, and composed for the occasion by the largest cricket in the band.

It was now the part of all, and permitted as well to the inhabitants of the Garden, to come up in order and be presented to the Queen, and to offer any gifts they might wish to bring. Two of the insects commonly called Walking-Sticks were in attendance, and were the ushers to announce each as they came up. It was proper that the Faeries should have the first place.

These came up in companies, according to their place in the procession. They where duly ushered into the presence of the Queen, and there was a spokesman for each party, who made a little address and offered a gift. The Faeries from the woods brought an anemone flower, set in dead forest leaf, and the spokesman explained that the flower was the anticipation of summer, and that it was fitting it should have such a back-ground. The Faeries from the streams were obliged to come sitting in shells filled with water and drawn by dragon-flies. They made a fine appearance and brought the scale of a trout; it was more beautiful than mother of pearl. The Faeries from the flags in the marshes brought a carpet made of leaves of the white violet; the central figure was a marsh mallow. The Faeries from the tops of the Firs brought a complete dinner service made of scales of the cone. The Faeries from the sea came upon the sea-foam, and the East Wind brought them. It made the place exceedingly chilly, and the Queen shivered. One could smell the saltness all over the Garden, and one of the Faeries was so overpowered by it that she fainted. They left their present, however, which was a necklace of crystal salt, and were off again. The Queen could not wear the necklace, however, for it made her head ache. The Faeries from the inside of caves came riding upon bats, and brought a stalactite made in the form of a horse of dandelion-down, for there is a favourite story among the Faeries in which such a horse figures. This was a very pretty piece of sculpture. The house Faeries brought a beautiful shawl made of the interwoven golden hair of the youngest child and the silver hair of her old grandfather. The church Faeries brought a sound from the organ; it was very solemn, and every one was quiet when it was offered. As for the gypsy Faeries they said they had nothing to give, and so would sing a song, which they did to the great delight of all, though the Walking-Sticks thought it not quite becoming.

The inhabitants of the Garden had been quite impatient for the Faeries to be through, for their turn was yet to come. It would be quite impossible to enumerate them all. The Flowers could not come themselves but they sent their choicest perfumes, and the Miller was so obliging as to carry for them a great many charming and delicate tints. The Bee gave a drop of honey, but he was so loud and coarse in his way and carried so many weapons about him that all were glad when he went. The Humming-Bird would not come, the Honeysuckle was his Queen, he said. The Red Ant said it was all fol-de-rol and there was no such thing as a faery in his opinion, much less a Queen Faery; and he stayed in the Hill and walked through all the passages to see that every thing was in order. The Butterfly, poor thing! was dead, and the Black Ant of course was too busy burying him to attend to such frivolous matters. The Grasshopper, however, came the whole length of the Garden, and each skip was precisely as long as the last. It took just one hundred and sixty-seven skips to reach the Lilac Bush. His uniform looked finely, and the Walking-Sticks rejoiced that here at last was one come who had style and observed etiquette. It was rather formal to be sure. The Walking-Sticks each bowed eleven times, and the Grasshopper raised his elbow so often and with so much precision, that you would have said it was very nicely calculated. He made a set speech which the Queen listened to, and then he passed out again; but he left no present, perhaps he thought he had honoured her enough by coming to pay his respects.

The Faeries agreed that the reception must be all over now and that the last of the inhabitants had come and gone; so they were ready for sport. They did not know—how should they? that the Earth worm was on the way; but he never reached the place in time; he was so blind that he lost the road frequently. Room was now made for a dance. The Fire-flies improved their lights and arranged them more artistically, and the Faeries took their places. The inhabitants of the Garden could only look on. Just as they were ready to begin, a bustling and confusion was observed among the group of house Faeries. What could be the stir? They were evidently very much excited, and the reason was this: One of their number, their spokesman at the reception, was leaning against a stalk of clover and looking up at the sky through the Lilac Bush. We think it hard to count the stars, they are so many in number, but to a Faery who once lived among them the stars are familiar as household faces. Thus the little Faery was aware of a new star that at that instant appeared in the sky. It was a very little star and rested between two larger ones, but it did not escape his quick eye and he was now all alive with excitement.

"We must lose no time!" cried he to his companions: "there is a new star! the child is born! come!" and they all sped to the house. One only remained for a moment to explain it to the Queen and then followed the rest.

The event produced great commotion in the Faery circle and all looked to the Queen to see what was to be done. The Queen instantly called her bugler, the tame Musquito, and bade him call the scattered Faeries all about her. So they came every one about the dandelion throne, and the herald of the Queen—the Fly in his blue coat, made proclamation that a child had been born and that it was a rare thing, and an excellent fortune both to Faeries and to the child, that it would be born upon the first day of the year. "Wherefore," he concluded, "let all the Faeries here gathered proceed as before and accompany the Queen to the place where the child lies, and let the gifts that have been brought to the Queen be carried by trusty servants."

So they set out as before in exactly the same order, except that the House-Faeries and the Sea-Faeries were not there. The Daddy-long-legs cleared the way to the door of the house, and the band of Crick ets played their sweetest air—'twas the Birth of the Daisy in fact. Arrived at the door the Daddy-long-legs took their place in lines upon each side of the step, and the Cricket band sate upon the scraper, for these might not enter. But the Faeries preceded by their Queen did enter, and their gifts went with them. They came into the room where little Janet lay. The House-Faeries were already there with hushed movements and ordering everything about the room. Around the bed gathered the hosts of Faeries—even the Faeries of the stream were there, a little drier than usual, though the House-Faeries made them keep on the outer circle.

The Queen was in the centre directly over little Janet. She bent nearer and nearer until she stood upon the forehead. She touched it with her lips, and that was the seal by which she signified that the newborn child of New-Year's Day was to be gifted with all that Faeries could give. The gifts which the Queen had received that night were freely offered to the little child. They were laid at her feet. None there saw them for none but the Faeries and the child could know of them. Each Faery, too, in the fulness of love and joy offered other gifts directly from their own nature; the Gypsy Faeries were very generous. They withdrew then and the Queen was left alone. She had her gift yet to bestow. "All of these," said she, "have richly endowed this child of New-Years Day." She looked at the gifts and knew that there was one thing wanting, yet she dreaded to bestow it. "It must be," she murmured, and kissing once more the brow of the child, dropped a tear upon it. Then she too left. The gifts were complete but the Queen was sad.

"She is a child of earth," she said, as she turned away; "it must be so."

The festivities of the day were finished and all was quiet in the Garden. The moon now rose and soon its light touched the Lilac Bush. At the touch the sweet perfume of the Lilac rose like a cloud of incense from the Bush. The air was filled with it, but the Bush was now deserted. "It was a great gift," it said, "that I should be permitted to have so much enjoyment. I am indeed happy, though twelve long months must pass before I bloom again, and these blossoms now upon me have lost their fragrance and shall fall to the ground. Yes, it is sweet to live, even though one's flowers die and one's fragrance is lost."

But the fragrance was not lost. It rose higher and higher; the clouds kept it not back and it ascended even to heaven.